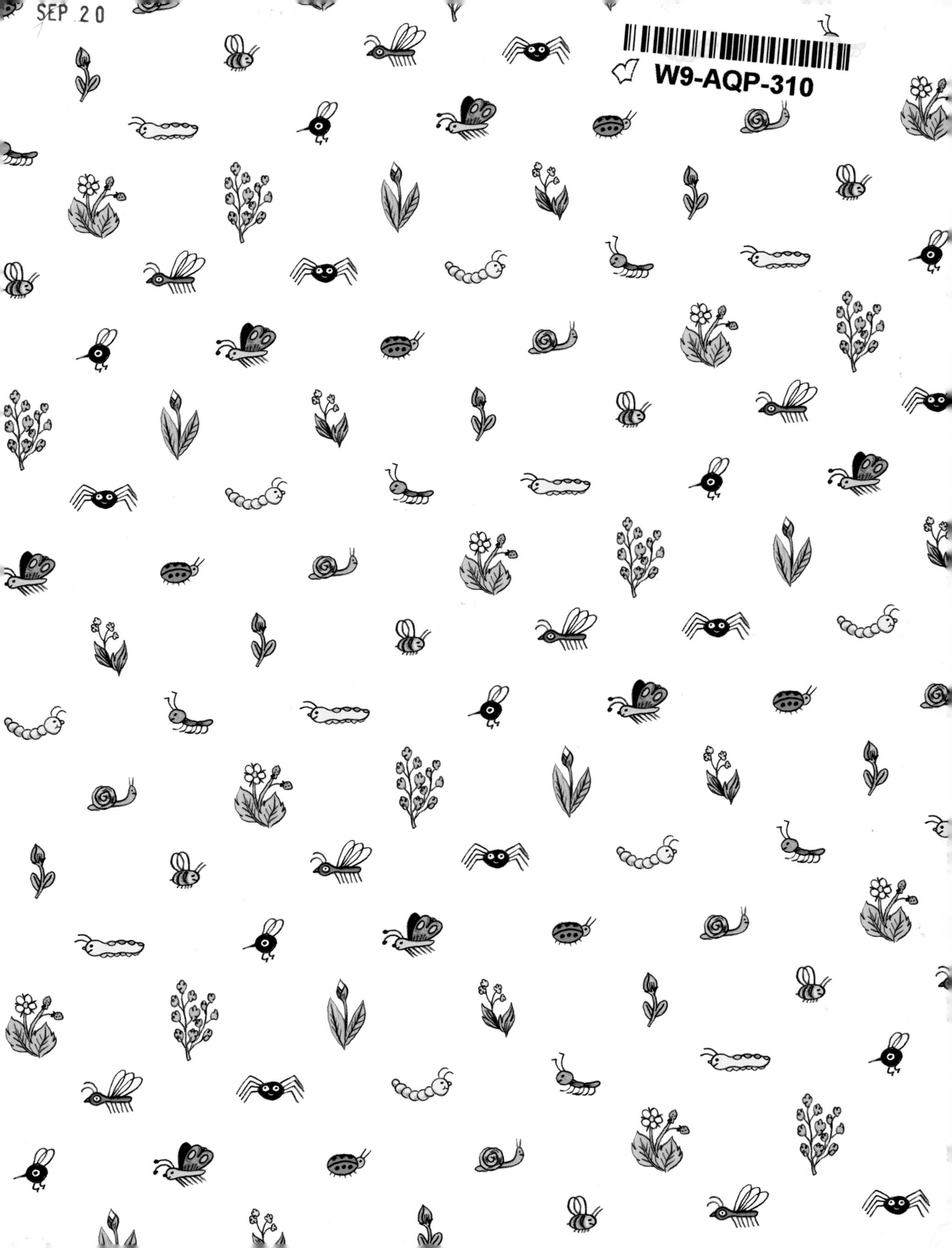

For Sylvie and Jean-Yves

First edition 2016

Published with the permission of Comme des géants inc.
CP 65006 BP Mozart
Montreal, Quebec, Canada

Translation rights arranged through the VeroK Agency, Barcelona, Spain

Published in English in 2018 by Owlkids Books Inc.

Published in French under the title *Mimose et Sam : Basilic en panique*

Owlkids Books acknowledges the financial support of the Canada Council for the Arts, the Ontario Arts Council, the Government of Canada through the Canada Book Fund (CBF) and the Government of Ontario through the Ontario Creates Book Initiative for our publishing activities.

Published in Canada by
Owlkids Books Inc.
1 Eglinton Avenue East
Toronto, ON M4P 3A1

Published in the United States by
Owlkids Books Inc.
1700 Fourth Street
Berkeley, CA 94710

Library and Archives Canada Cataloguing in Publication

Cathon, 1990-
[Mimose & Sam. English]
Poppy & Sam and the leaf thief / Cathon.

Translated by Karen Li.
Translation of: Mimose & Sam, Basilic en panique.
ISBN 978-1-77147-329-3 (hardcover)

I. Title. II. Title: Poppy and Sam and the leaf thief.
III. Title: Mimose & Sam. English.

PS8605.A8786M5513 2018 jC843'.6 C2017-907426-1

Library of Congress Control Number: 2017961369

ONTARIO ARTS COUNCIL
CONSEIL DES ARTS DE L'ONTARIO
an Ontario government agency
un organisme du gouvernement de l'Ontario

Canada Council for the Arts
Conseil des Arts du Canada

Canada

Manufactured in Shenzhen, Guangdong, China, in April 2019, by WKT Co. Ltd.
Job #18CB3975

B C D E F G

Publisher of Chirp, Chickadee and OWL
www.owlkidsbooks.com
Owlkids Books is a division of bayard canada

POPPY & SAM
AND THE LEAF THIEF

By CATHON

Owlkids Books

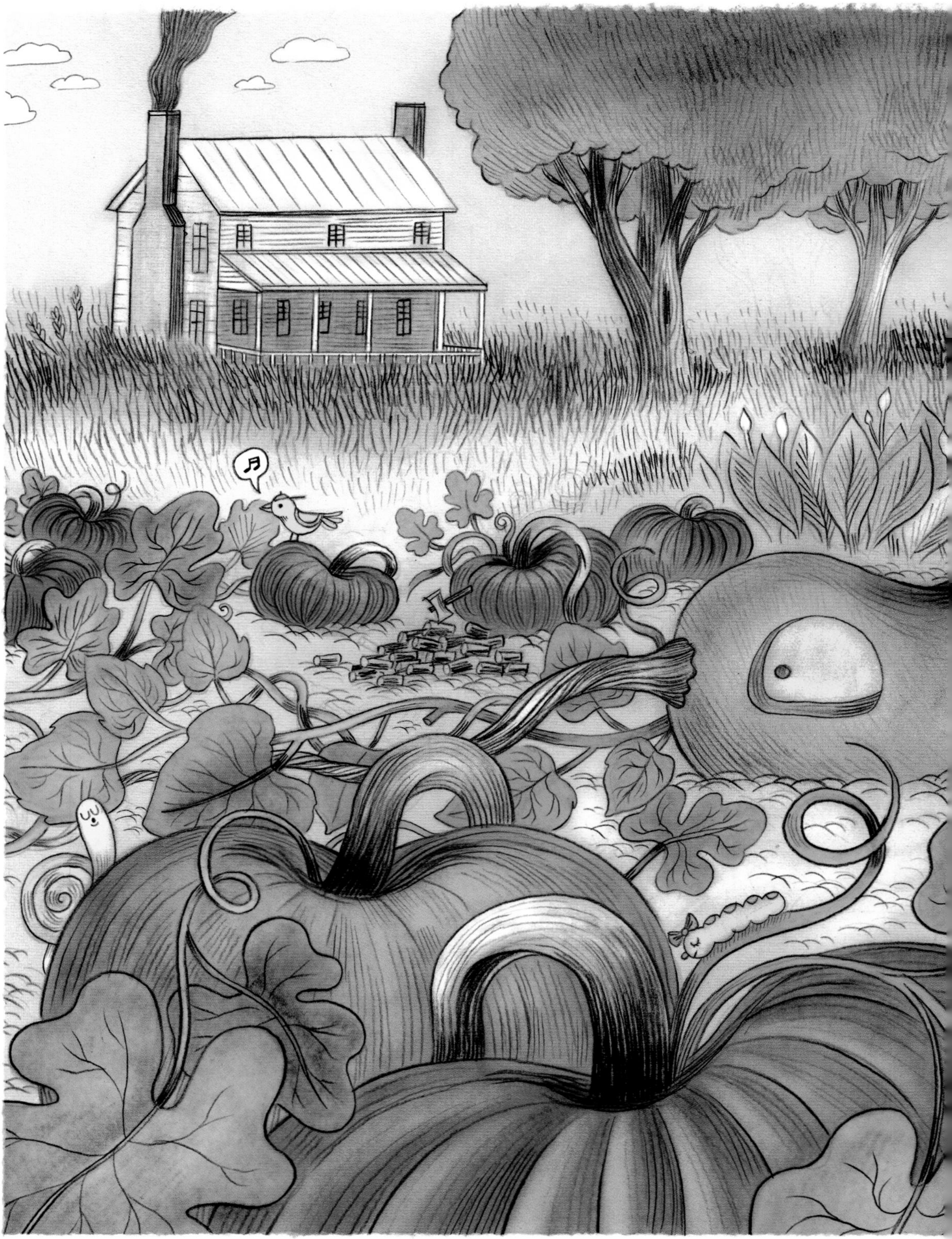

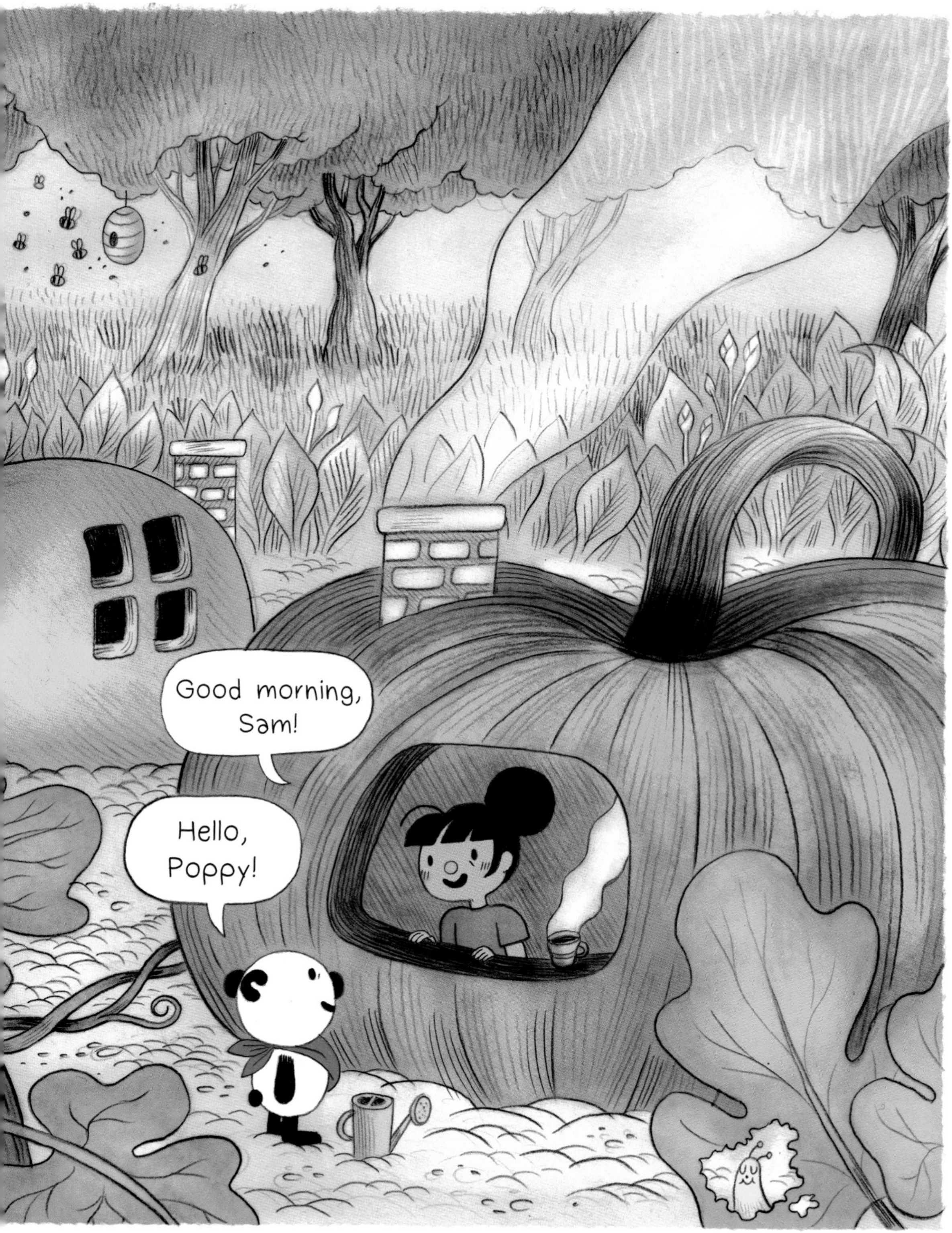
Good morning, Sam!
Hello, Poppy!

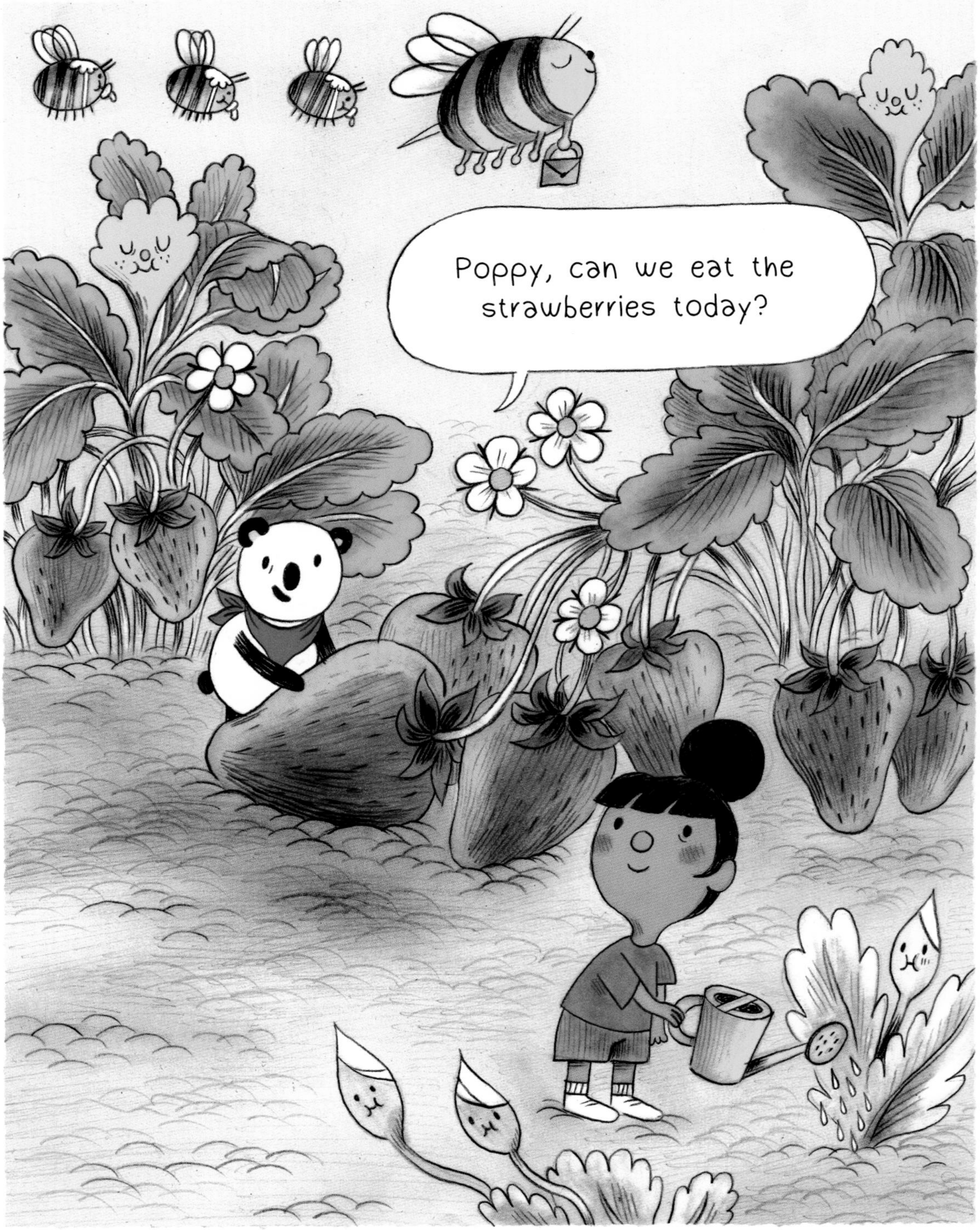
Poppy, can we eat the strawberries today?

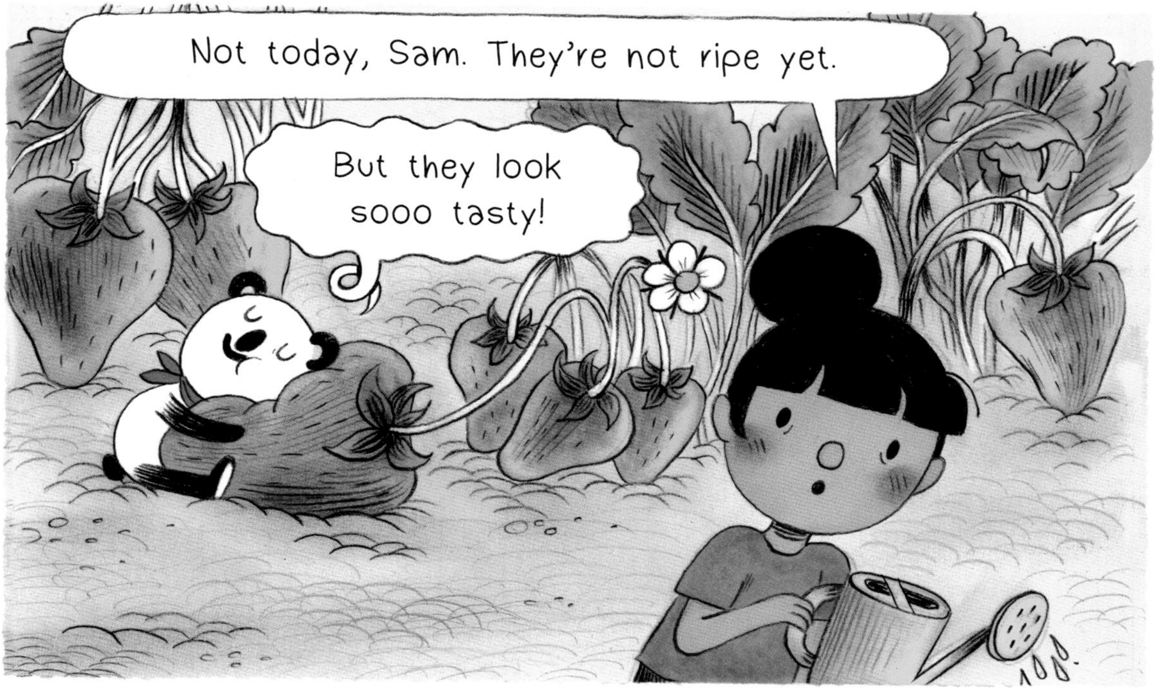
Not today, Sam. They're not ripe yet.
But they look sooo tasty!

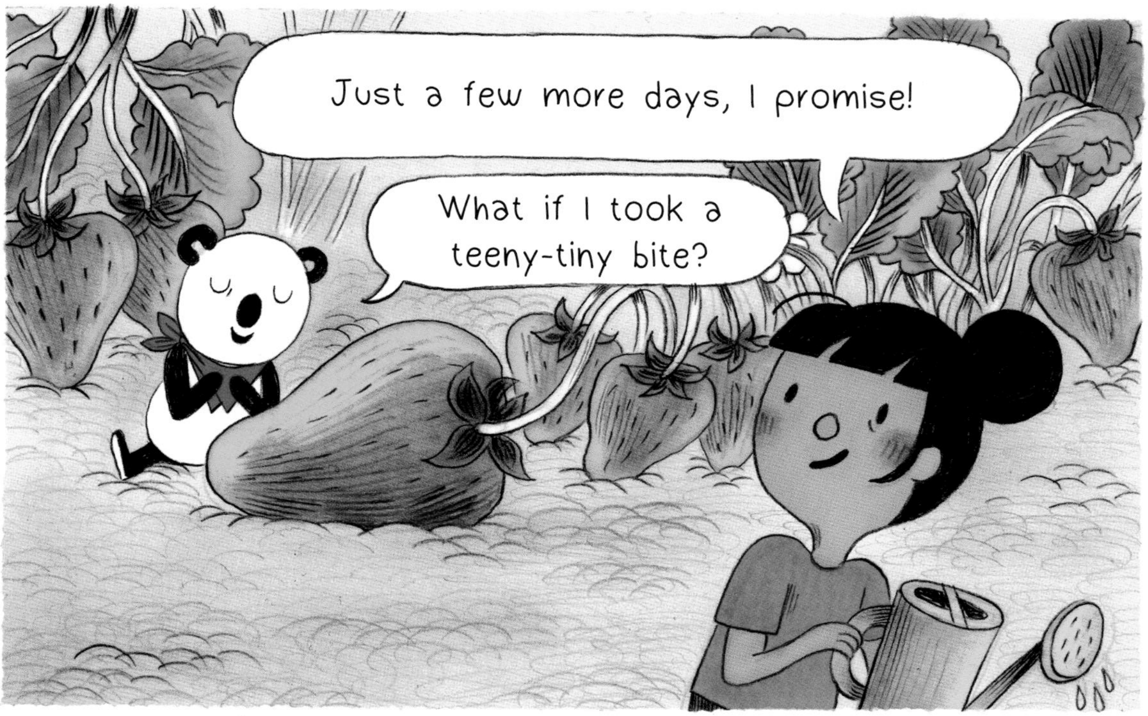
Just a few more days, I promise!
What if I took a teeny-tiny bite?

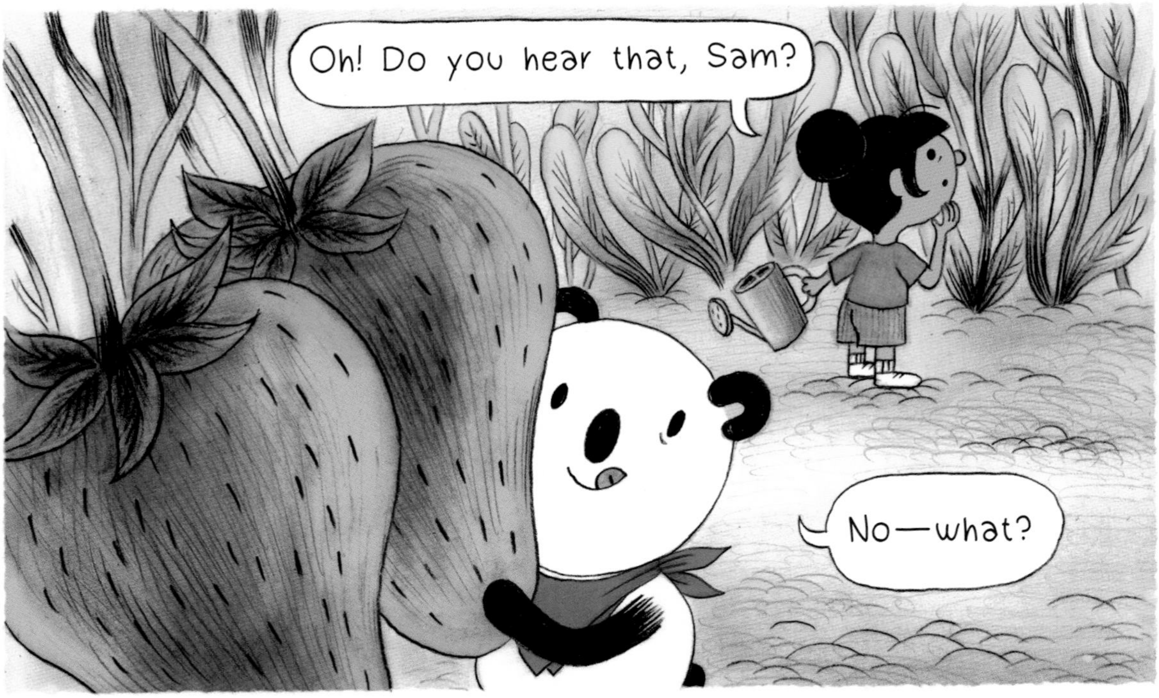
Oh! Do you hear that, Sam?
No—what?

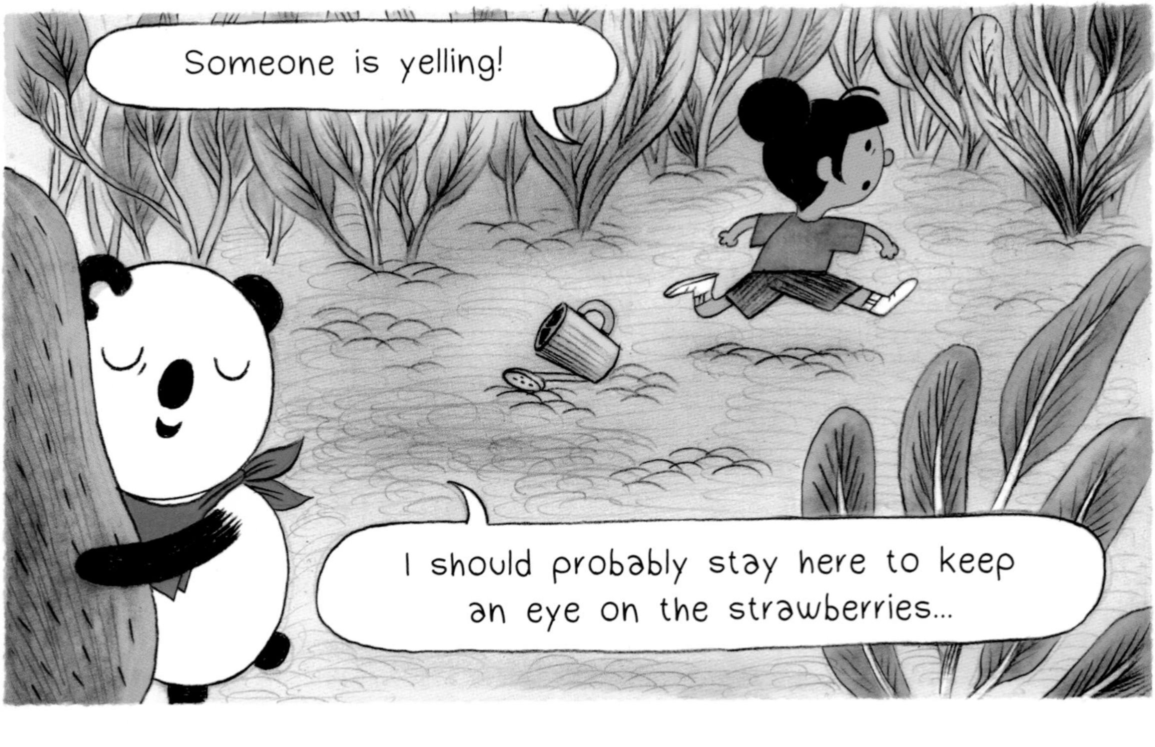
Someone is yelling!
I should probably stay here to keep an eye on the strawberries...

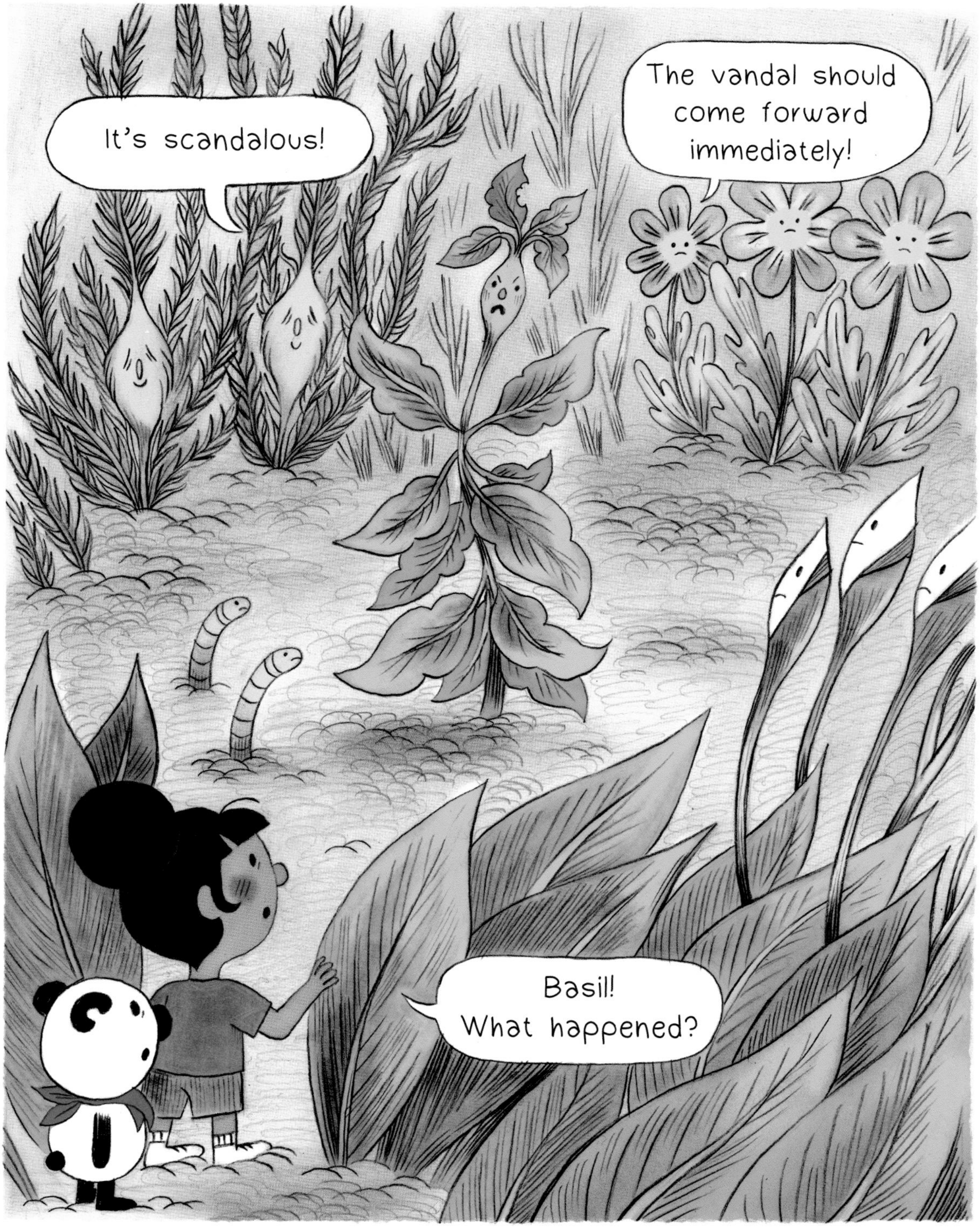
It's scandalous!
The vandal should come forward immediately!
Basil! What happened?

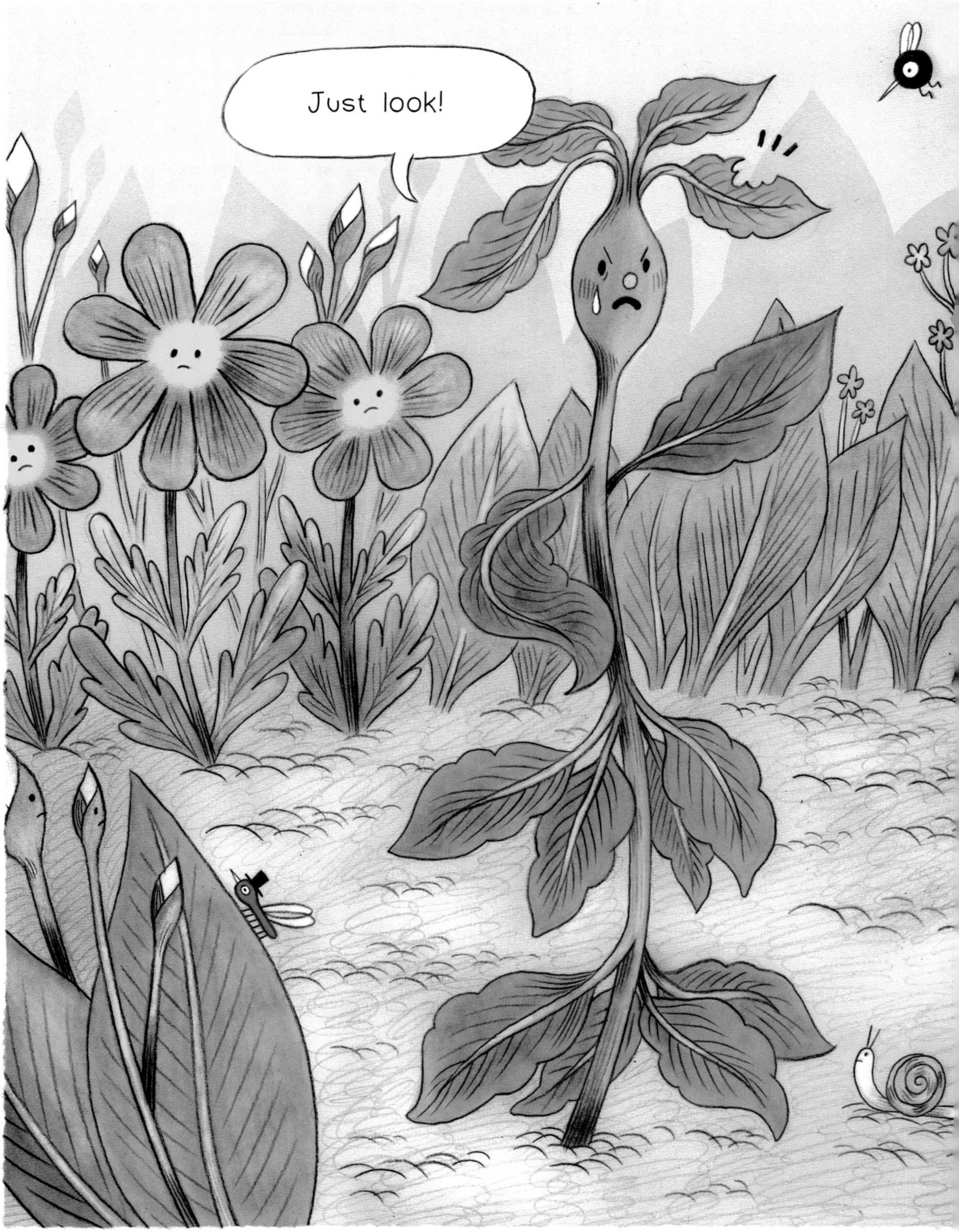
Just look!

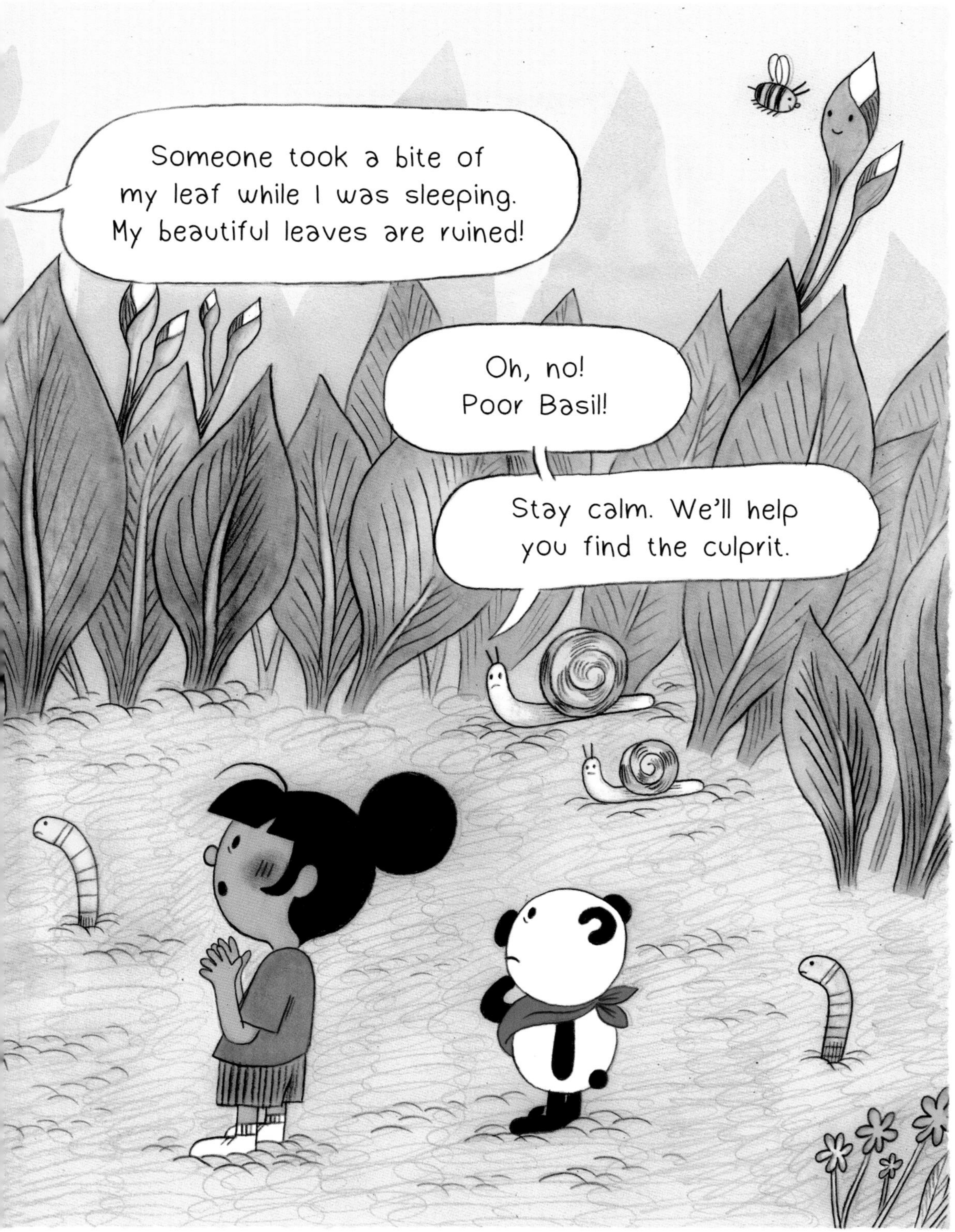
Someone took a bite of my leaf while I was sleeping. My beautiful leaves are ruined!
Oh, no! Poor Basil!
Stay calm. We'll help you find the culprit.

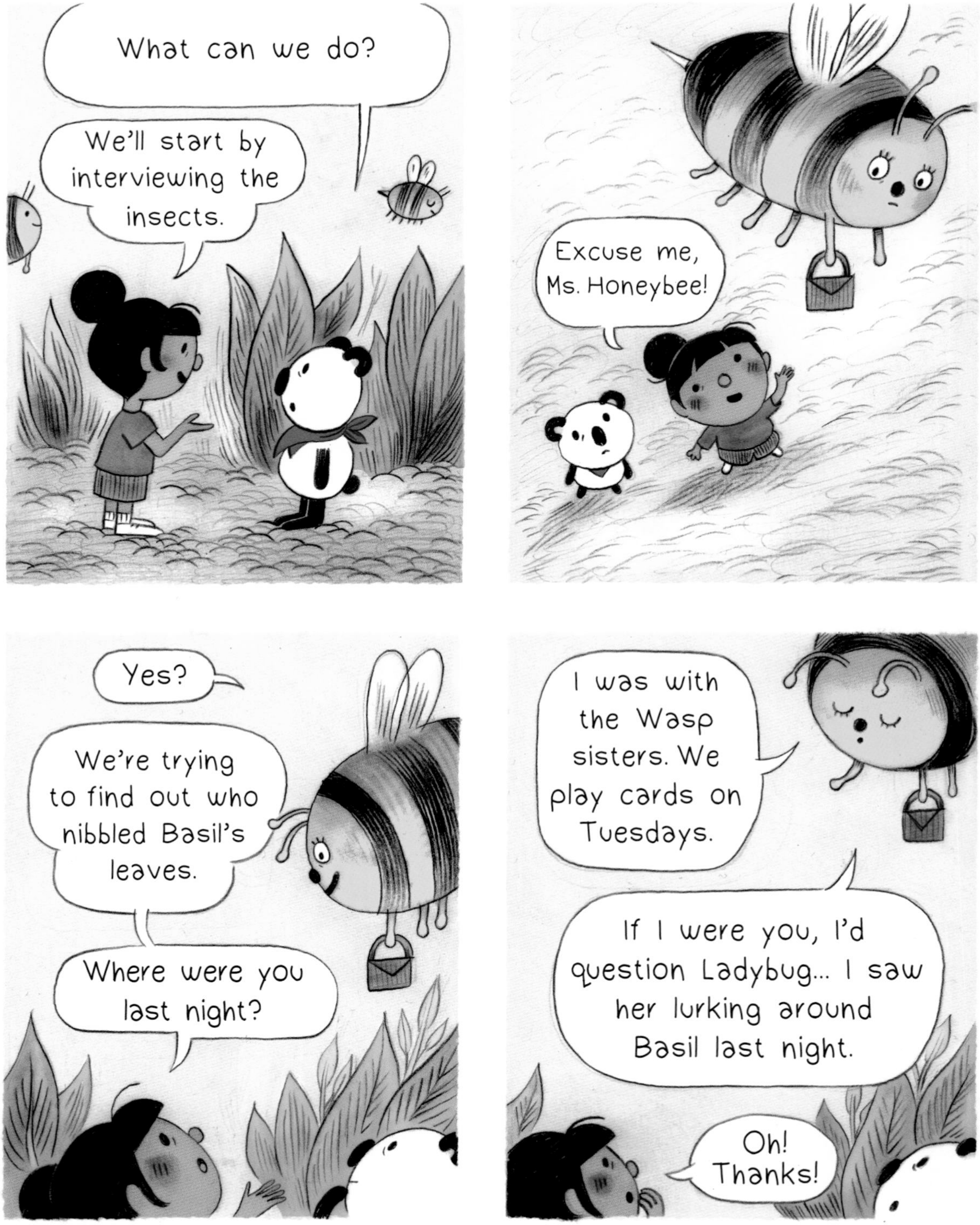
What can we do?
We'll start by interviewing the insects.
Excuse me, Ms. Honeybee!
Yes?
We're trying to find out who nibbled Basil's leaves.
Where were you last night?
I was with the Wasp sisters. We play cards on Tuesdays.
If I were you, I'd question Ladybug... I saw her lurking around Basil last night.
Oh! Thanks!

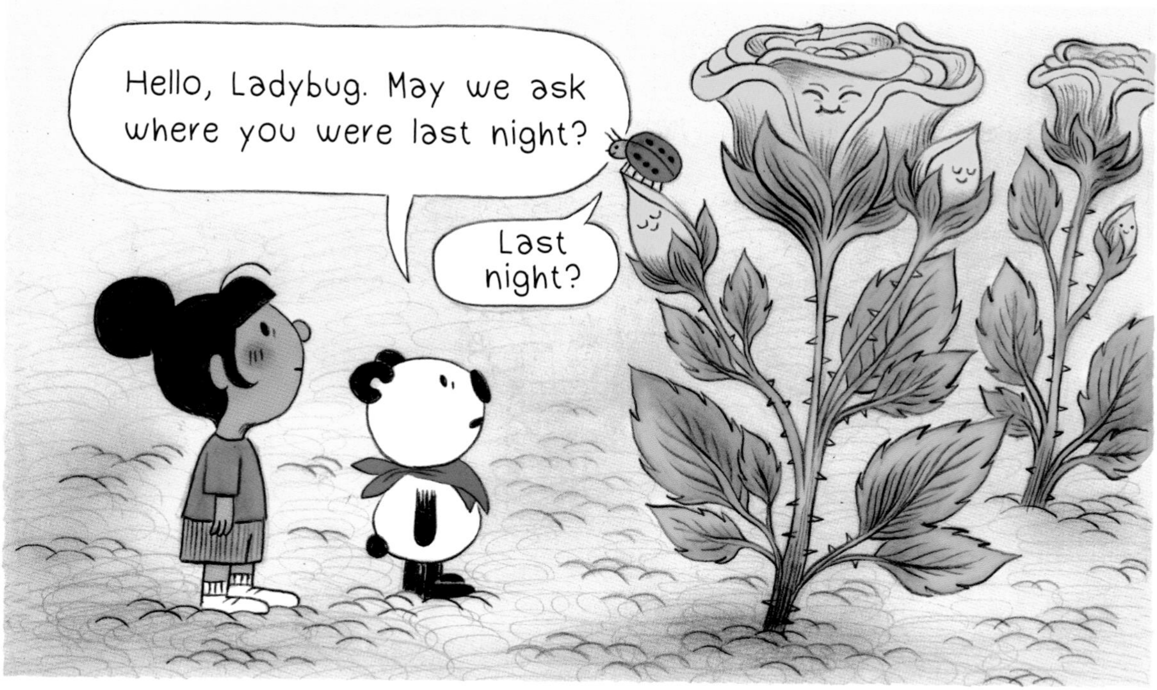
Hello, Ladybug. May we ask where you were last night?
Last night?

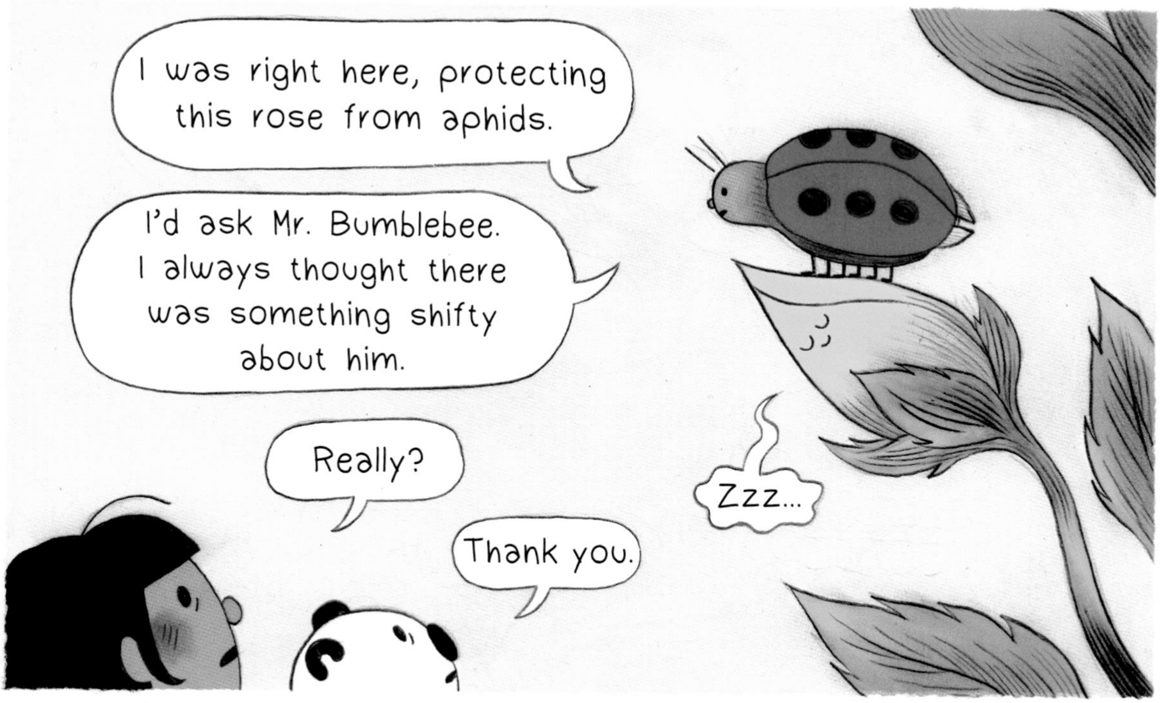
I was right here, protecting this rose from aphids.
I'd ask Mr. Bumblebee. I always thought there was something shifty about him.
Really?
Thank you.
Zzz...

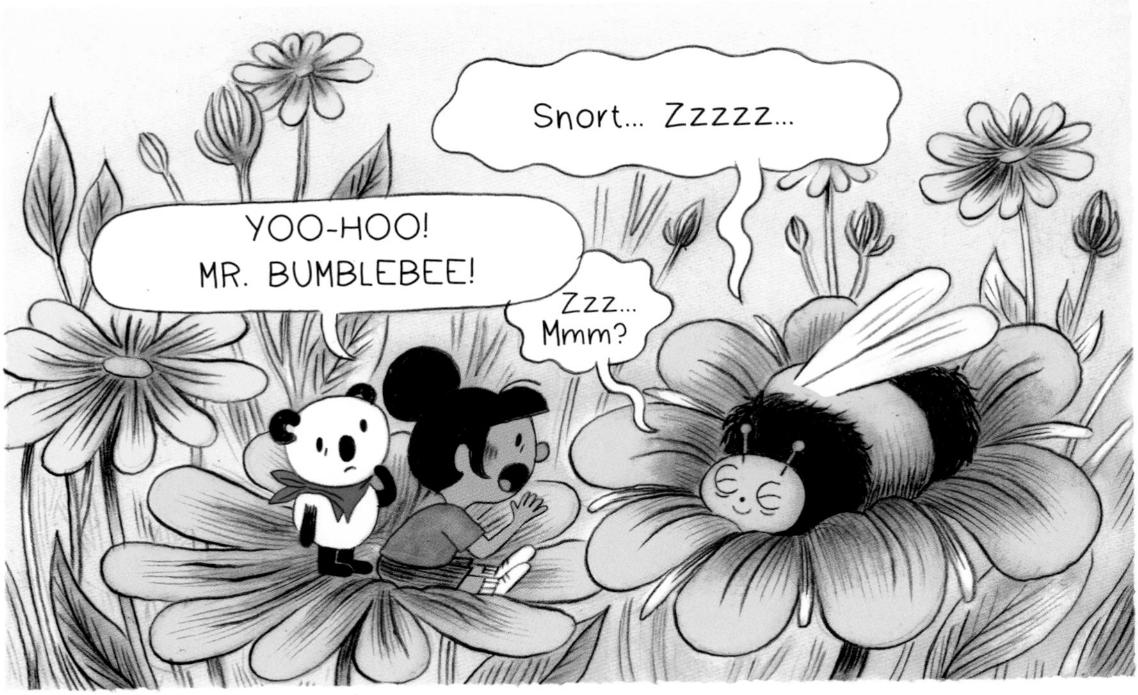
YOO-HOO! MR. BUMBLEBEE!
Snort... Zzzzz...
Zzz... Mmm?

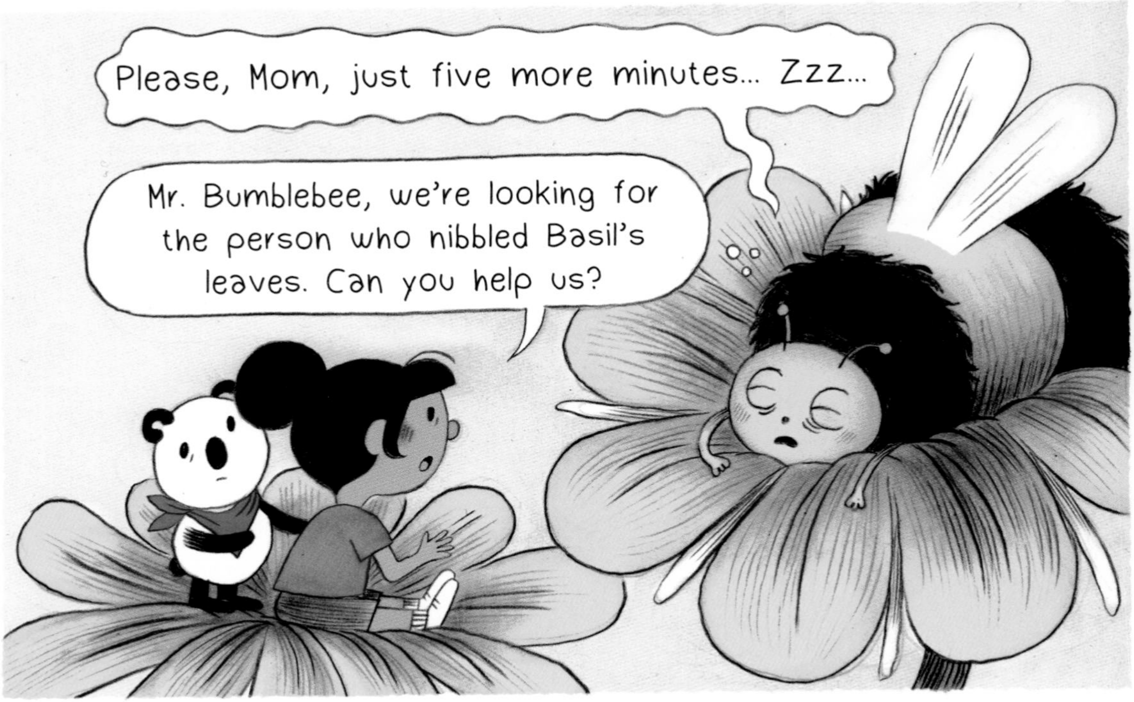
Please, Mom, just five more minutes... Zzz...
Mr. Bumblebee, we're looking for the person who nibbled Basil's leaves. Can you help us?

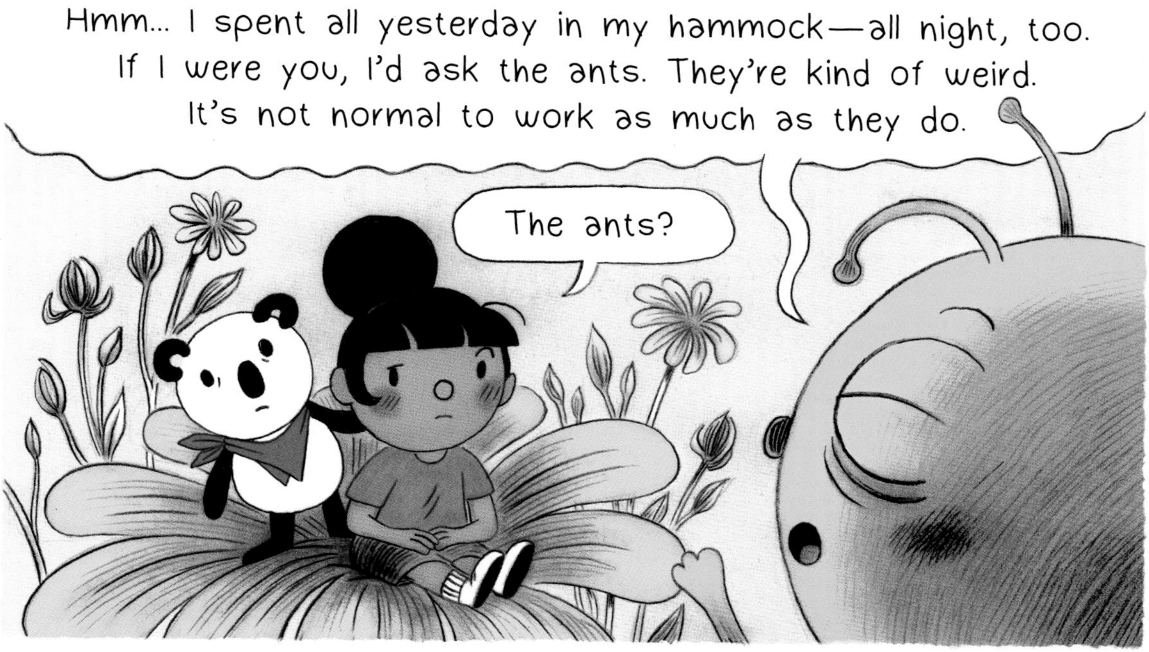
Hmm... I spent all yesterday in my hammock—all night, too. If I were you, I'd ask the ants. They're kind of weird. It's not normal to work as much as they do.
The ants?

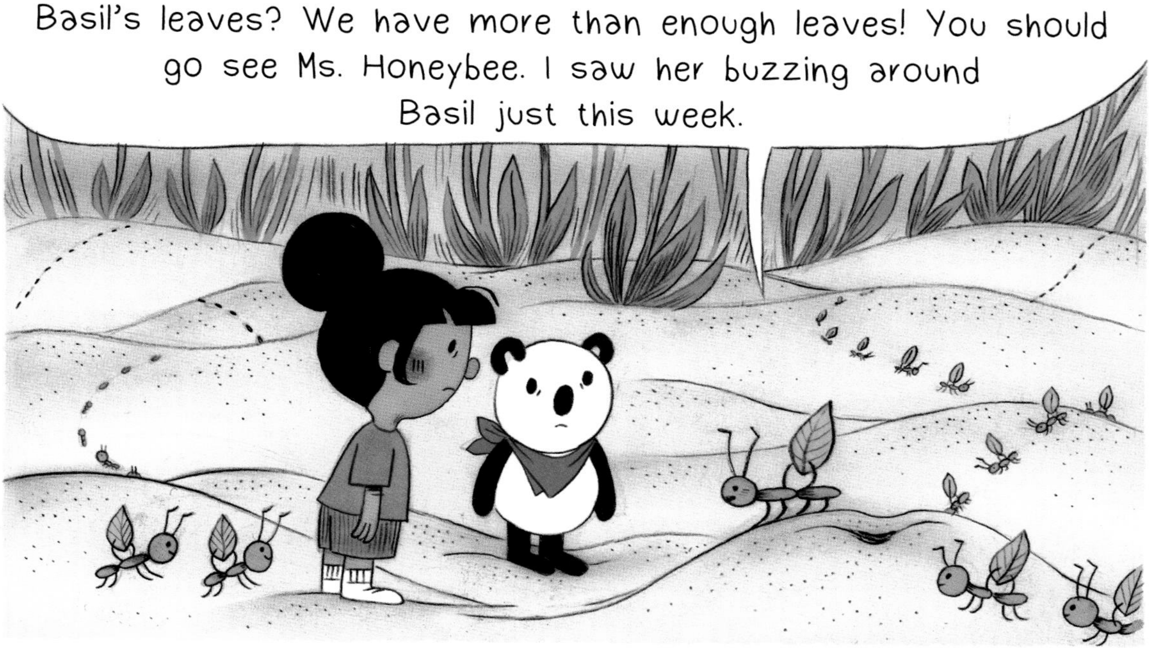
Basil's leaves? We have more than enough leaves! You should go see Ms. Honeybee. I saw her buzzing around Basil just this week.

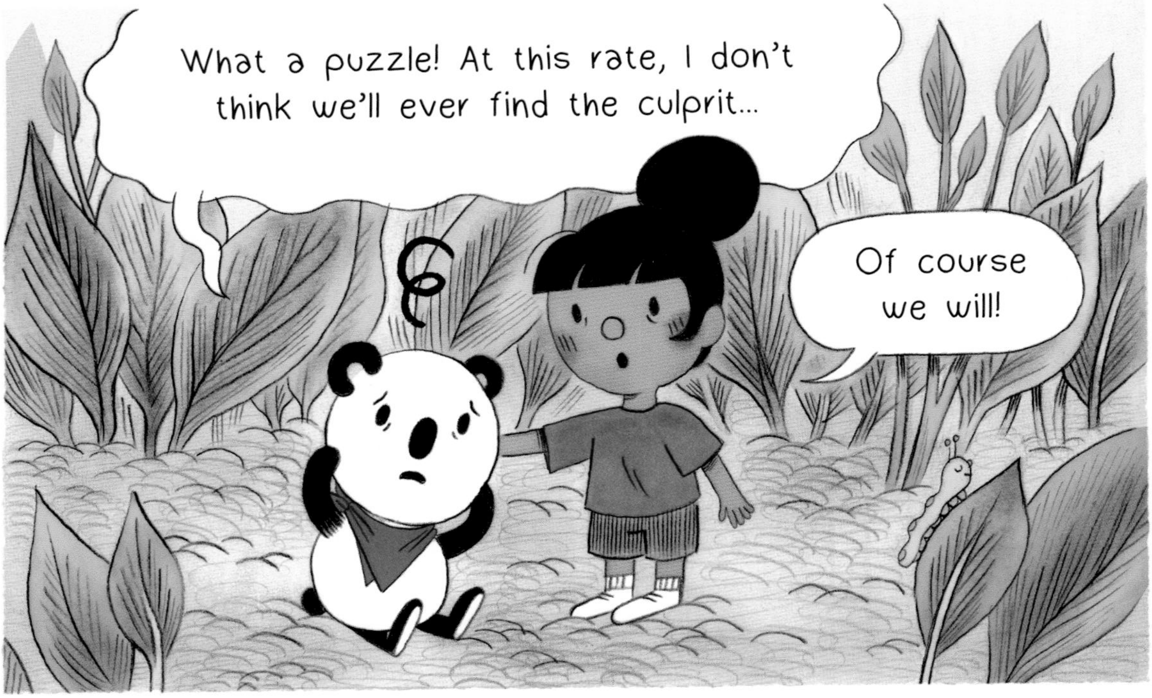
What a puzzle! At this rate, I don't think we'll ever find the culprit...
Of course we will!

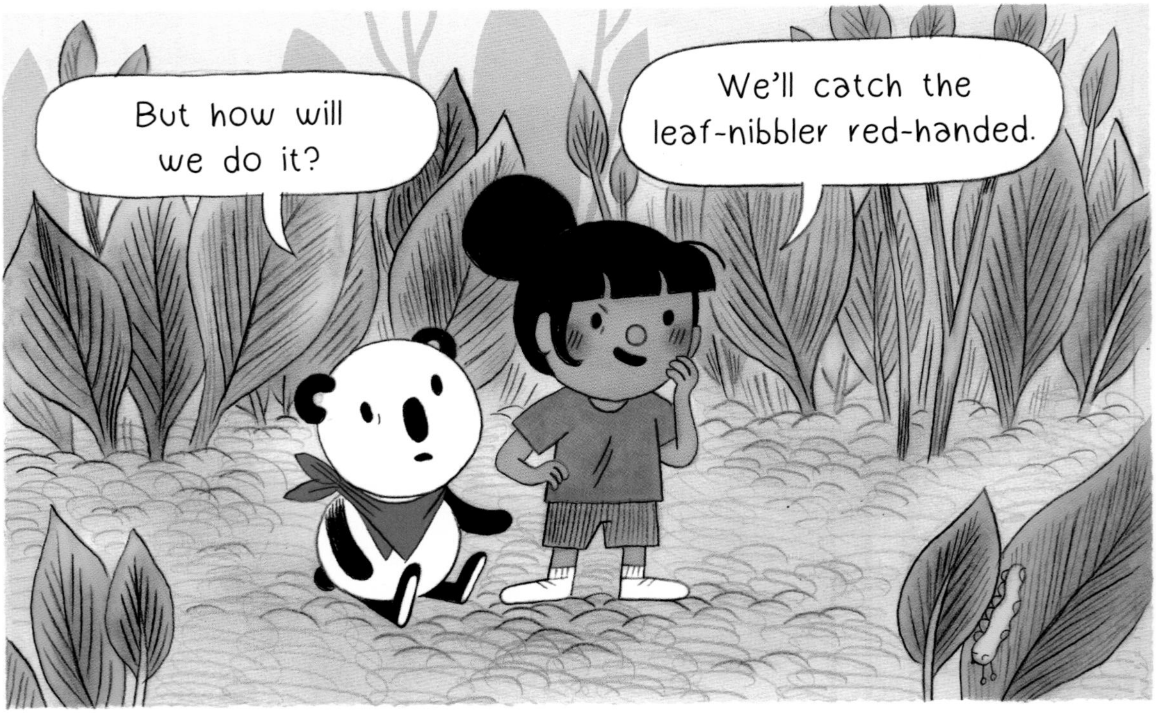
But how will we do it?
We'll catch the leaf-nibbler red-handed.

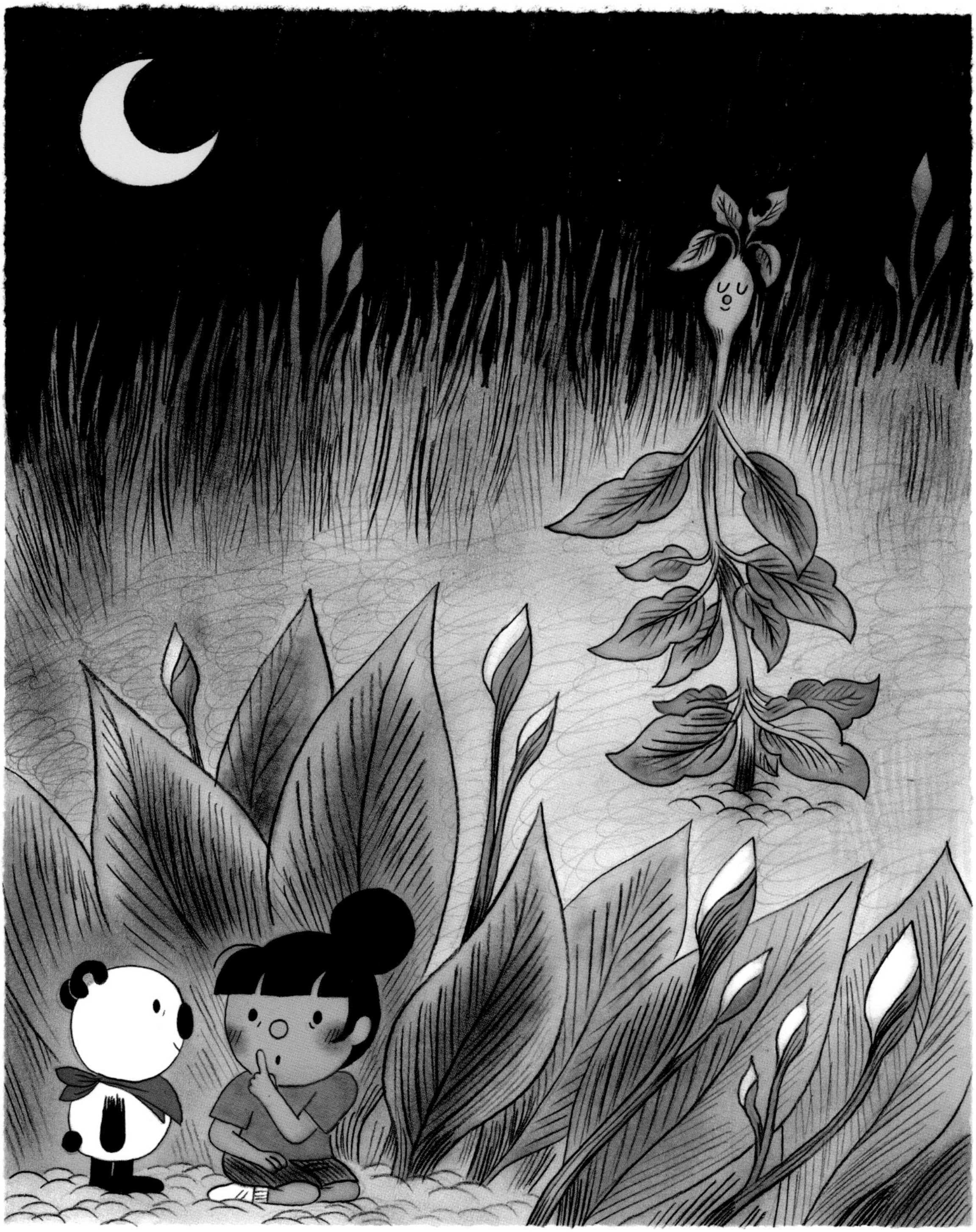

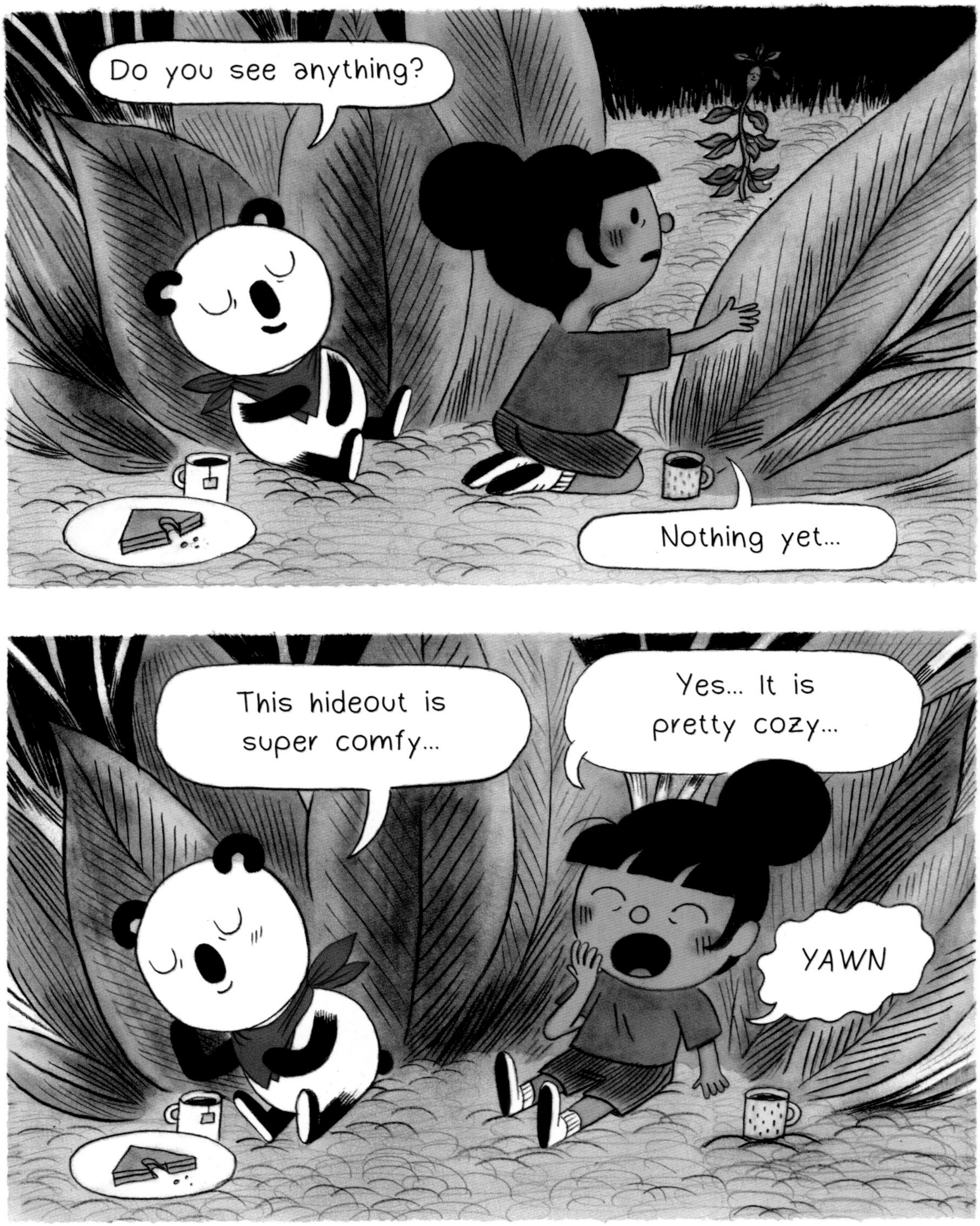

Do you see anything?
Nothing yet...
This hideout is super comfy...
Yes... It is pretty cozy...
YAWN

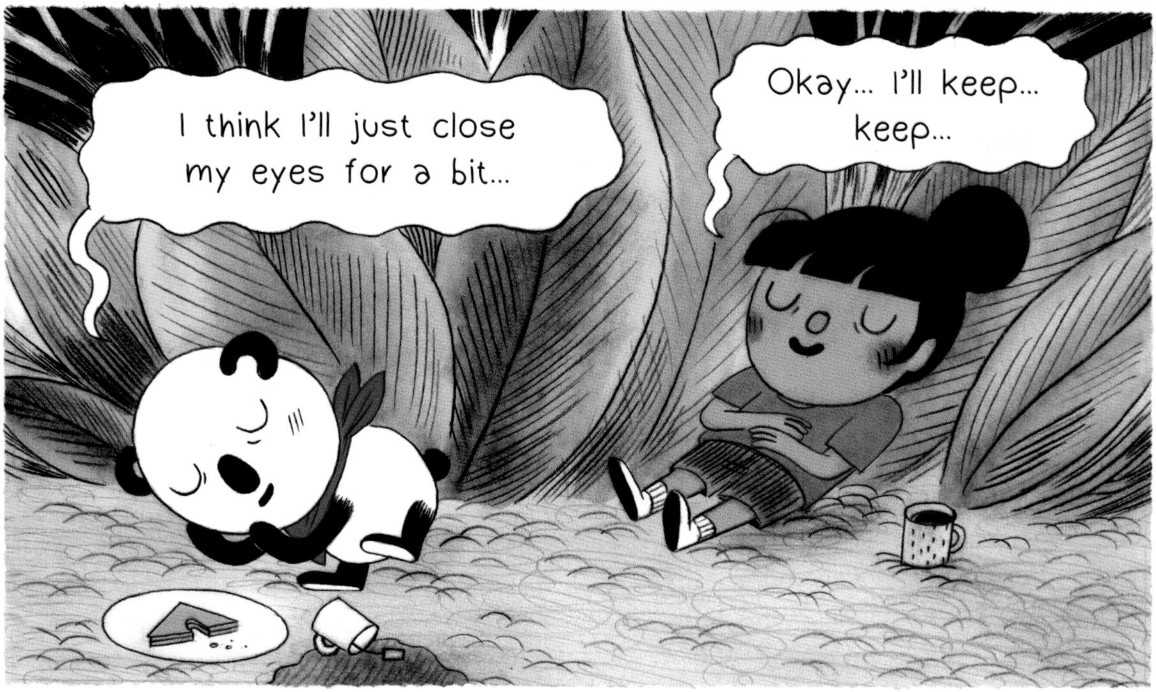
I think I'll just close my eyes for a bit...
Okay... I'll keep... keep...

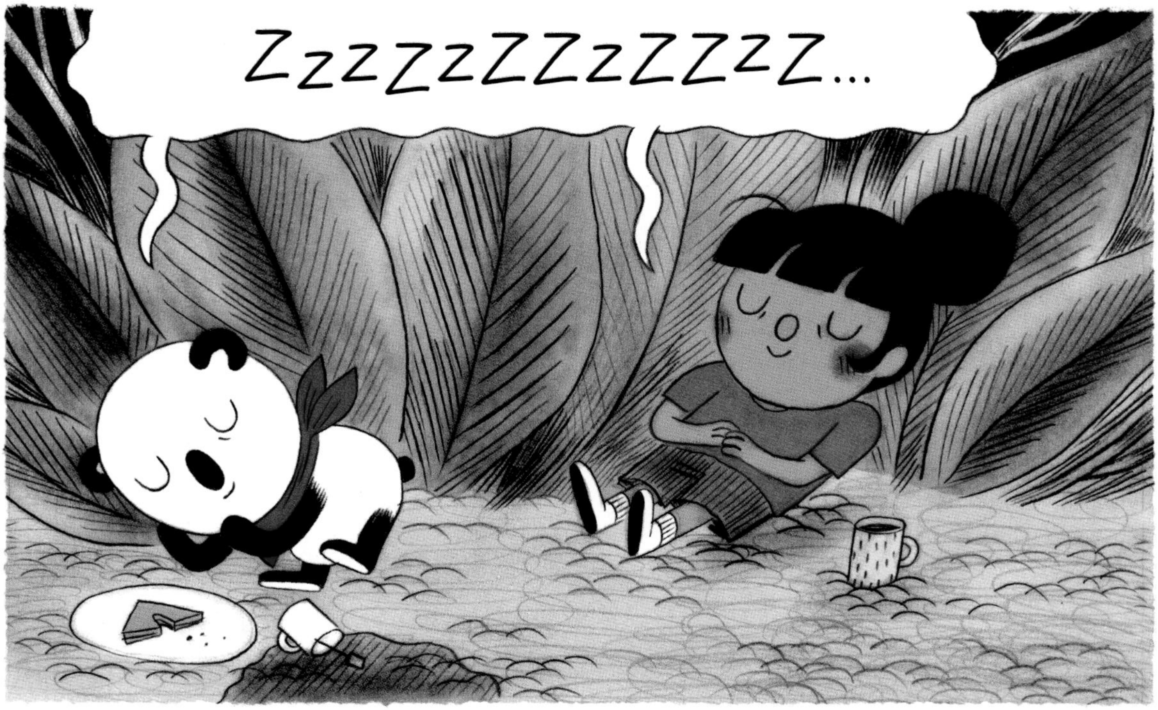
ZzzzZzzZZZzZZzzZ...

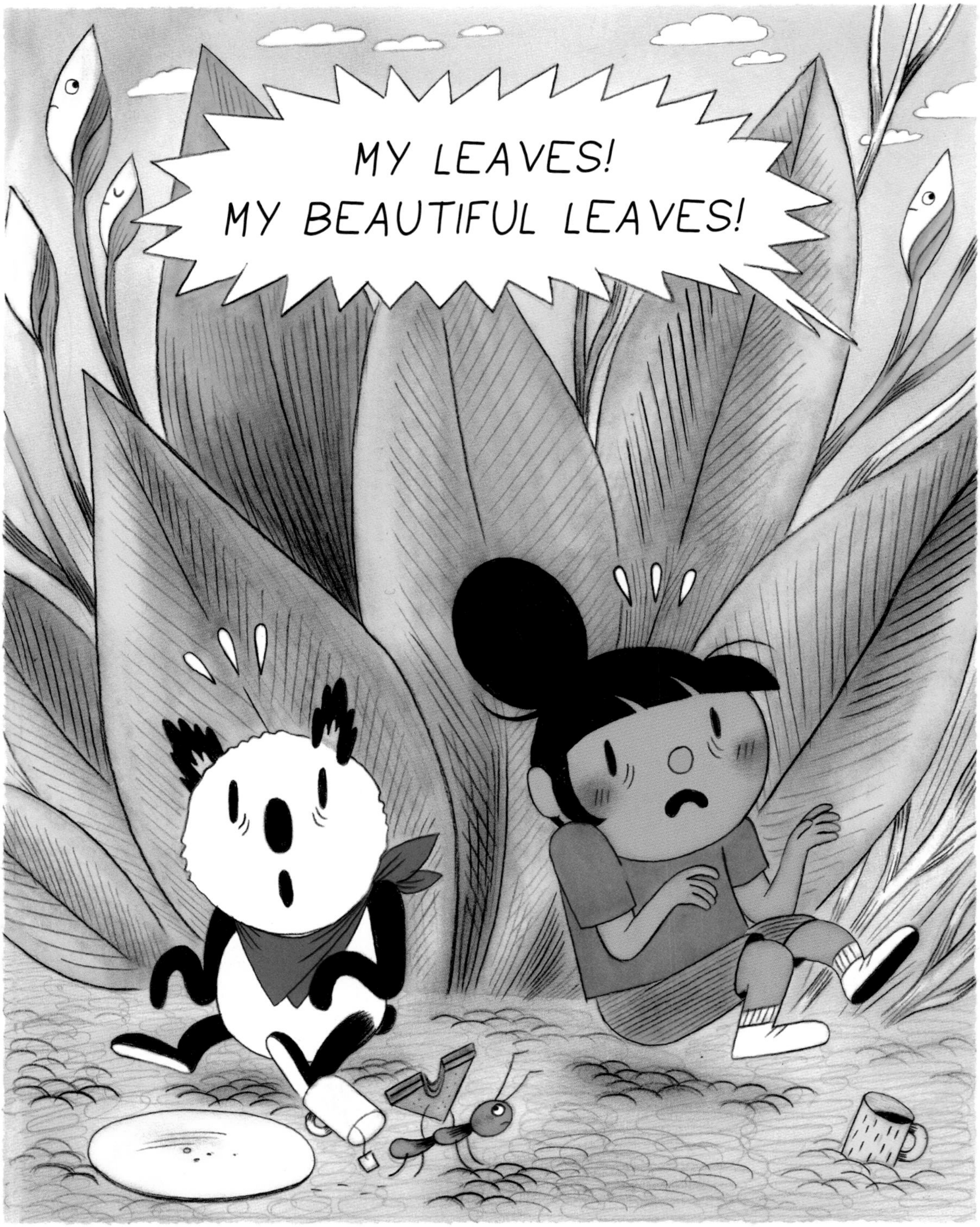
MY LEAVES!
MY BEAUTIFUL LEAVES!

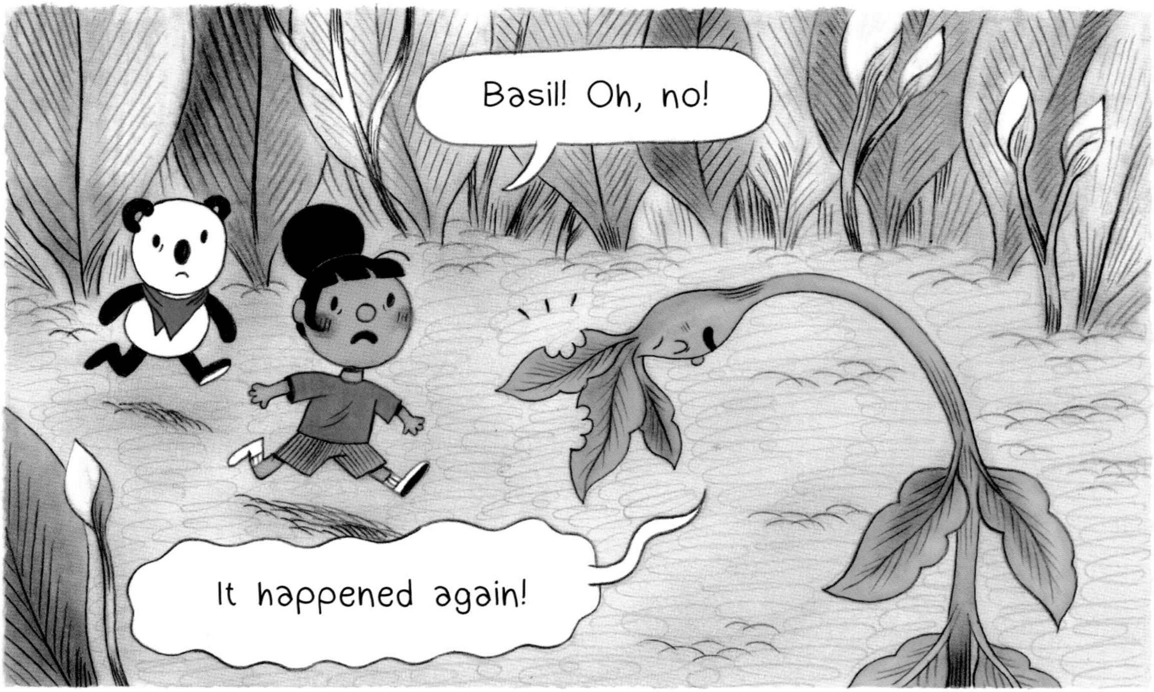
Basil! Oh, no!
It happened again!

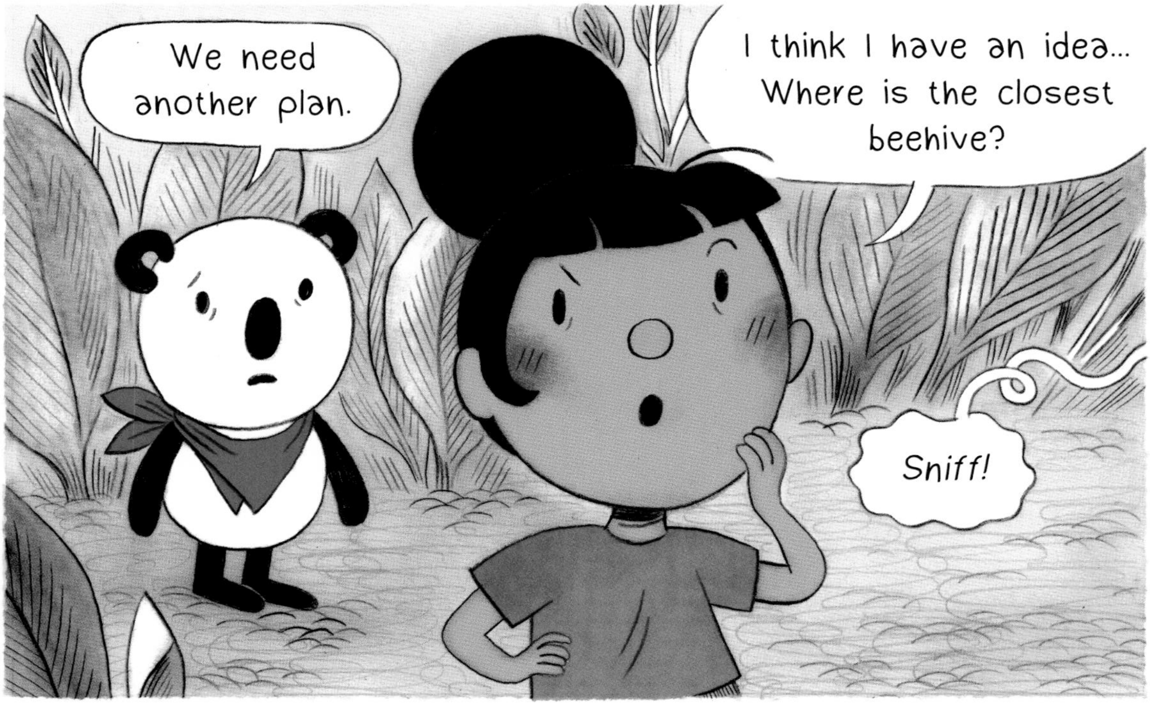
We need another plan.
I think I have an idea... Where is the closest beehive?
Sniff!

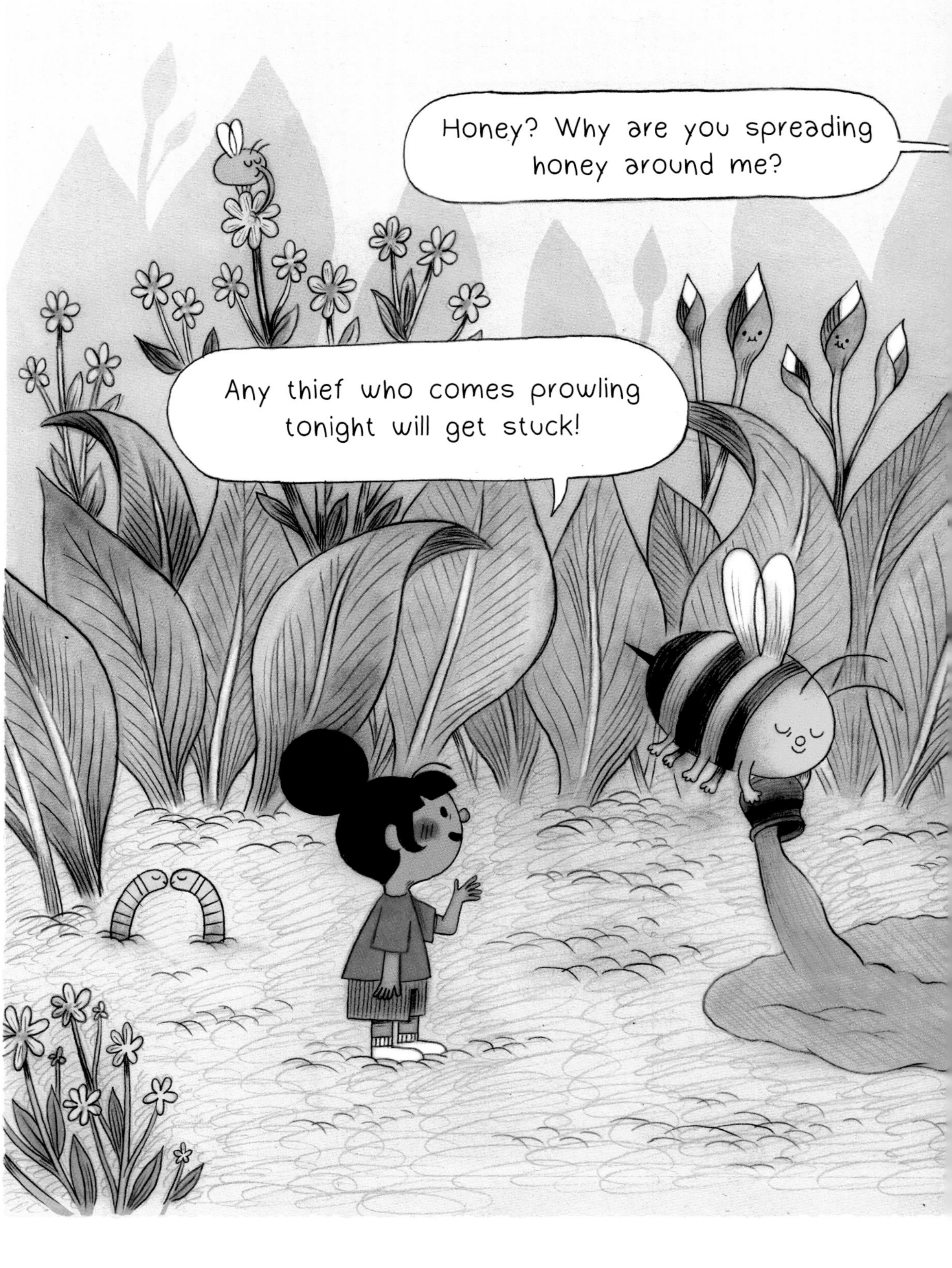
Honey? Why are you spreading honey around me?
Any thief who comes prowling tonight will get stuck!

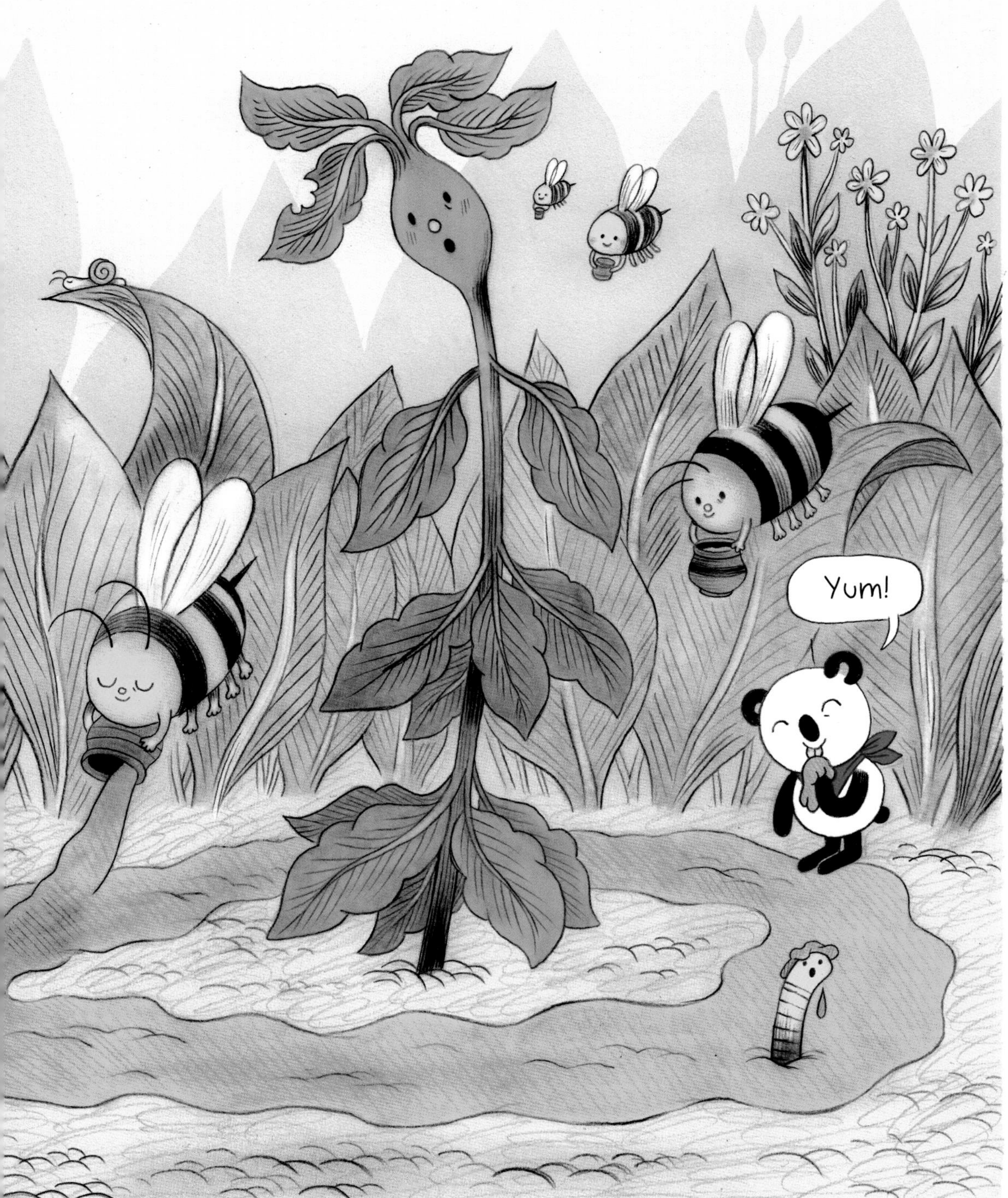
Yum!

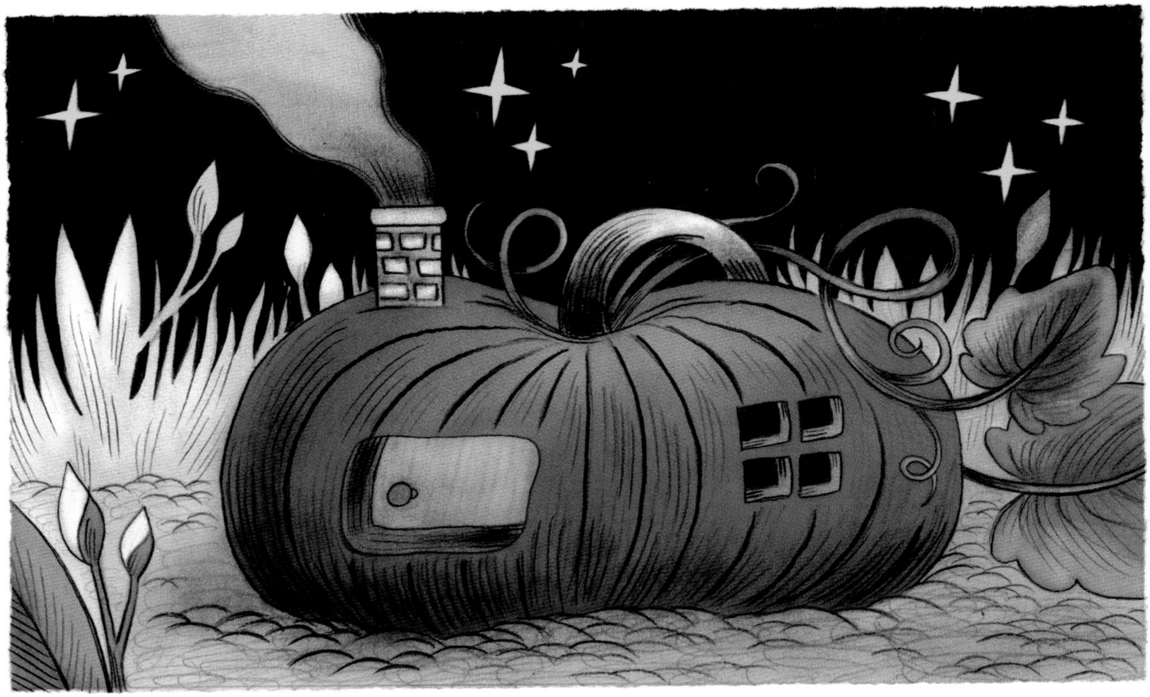

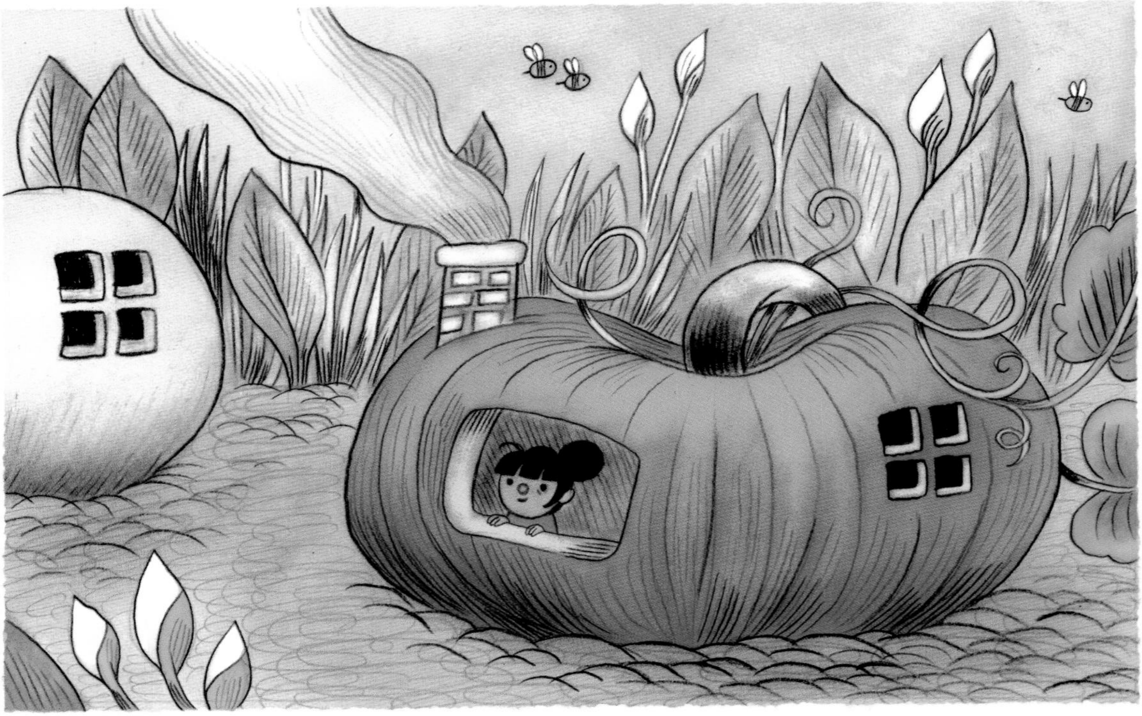

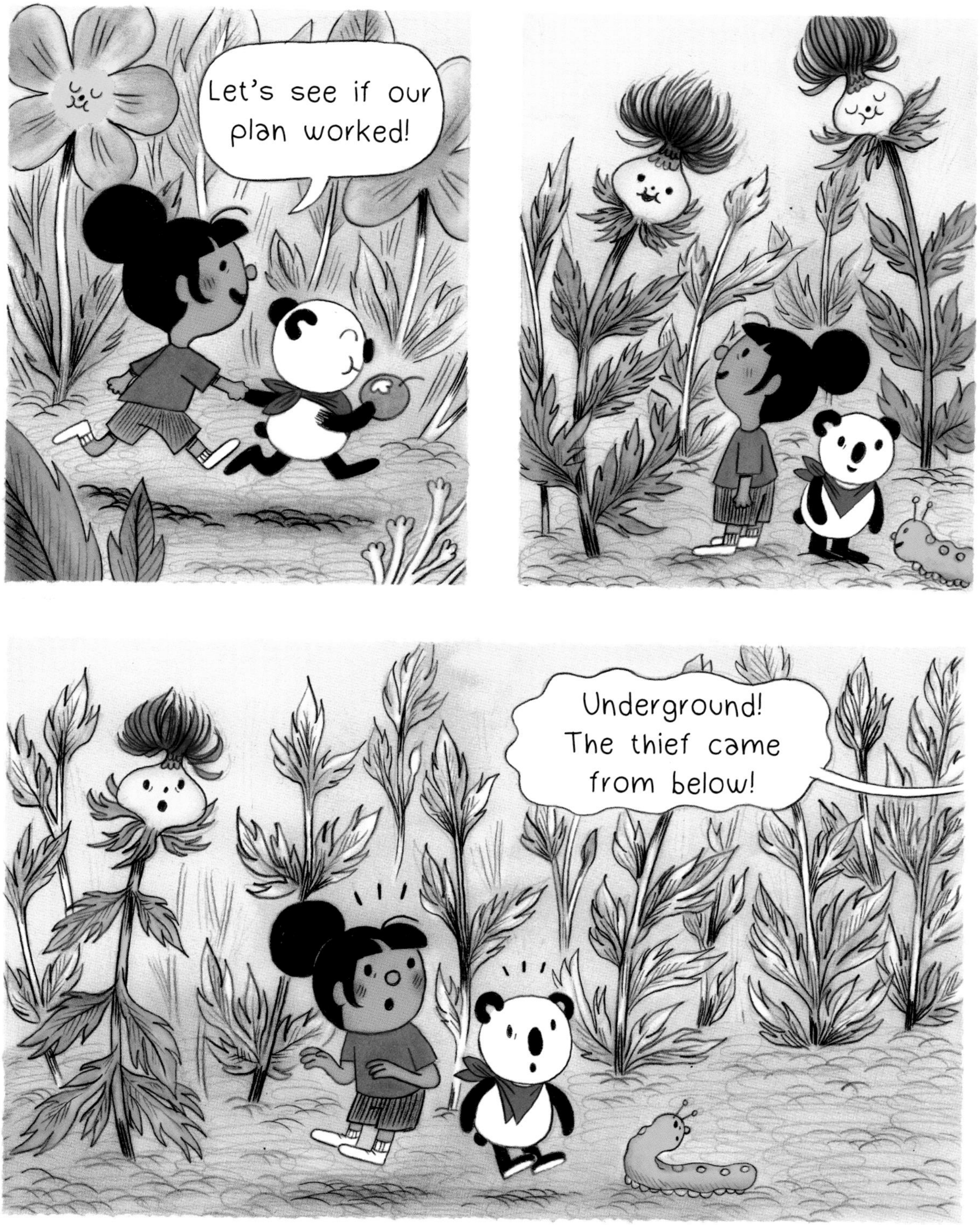
Let's see if our plan worked!
Underground! The thief came from below!

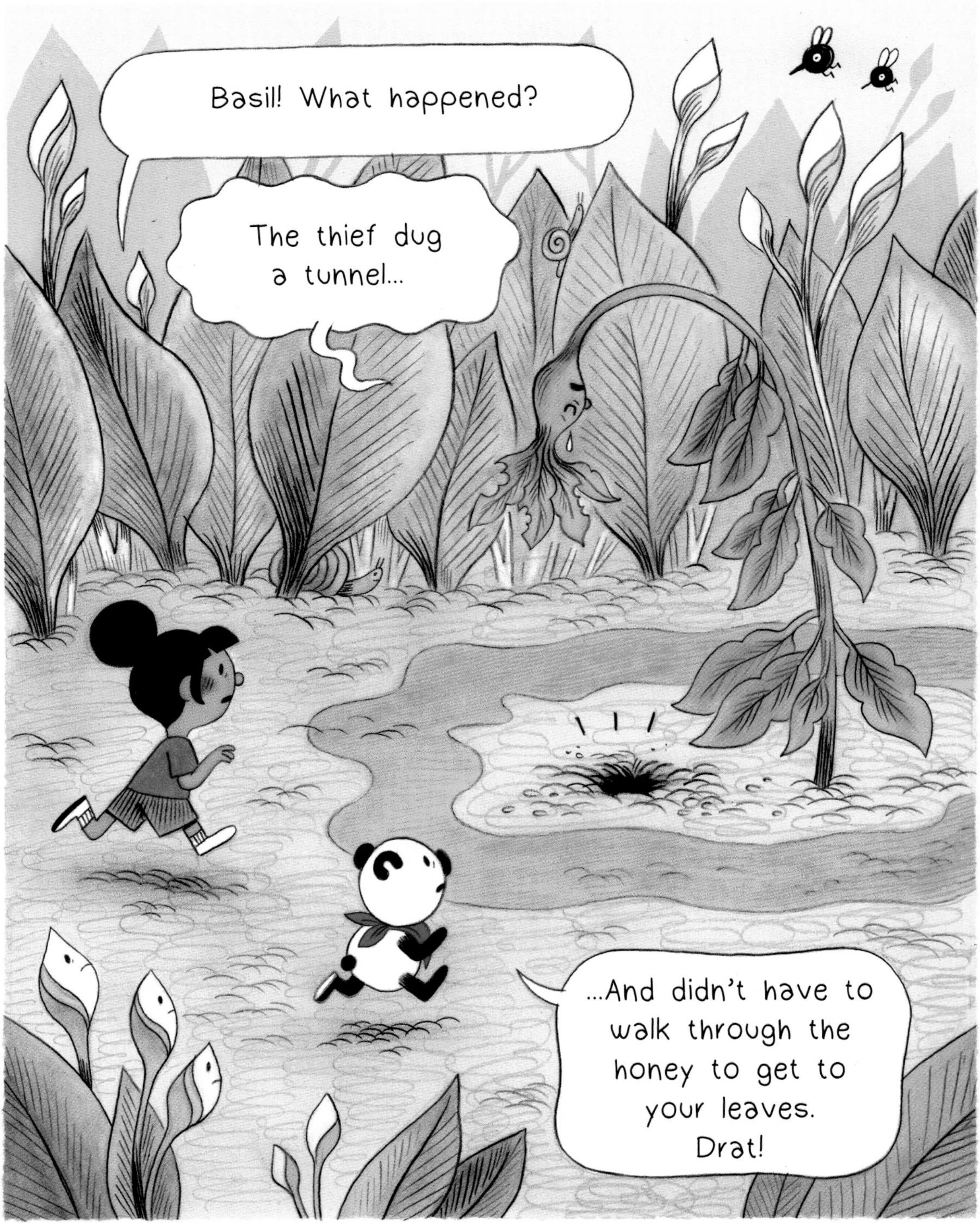
Basil! What happened?
The thief dug a tunnel...
...And didn't have to walk through the honey to get to your leaves. Drat!

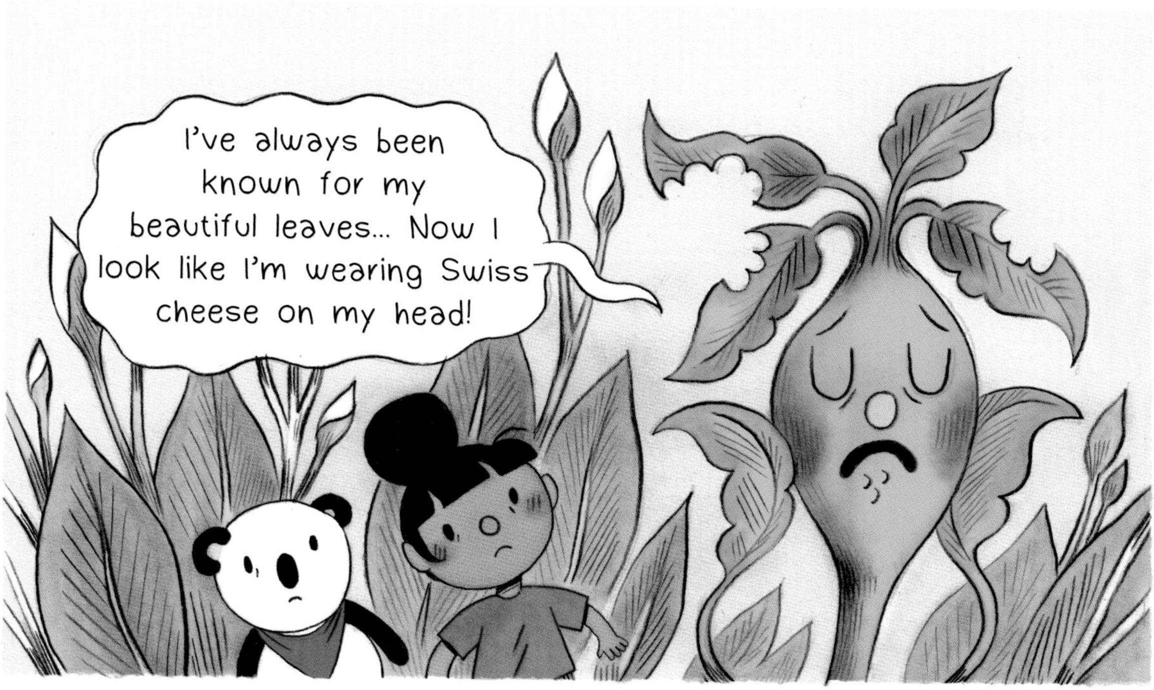
I've always been known for my beautiful leaves... Now I look like I'm wearing Swiss cheese on my head!

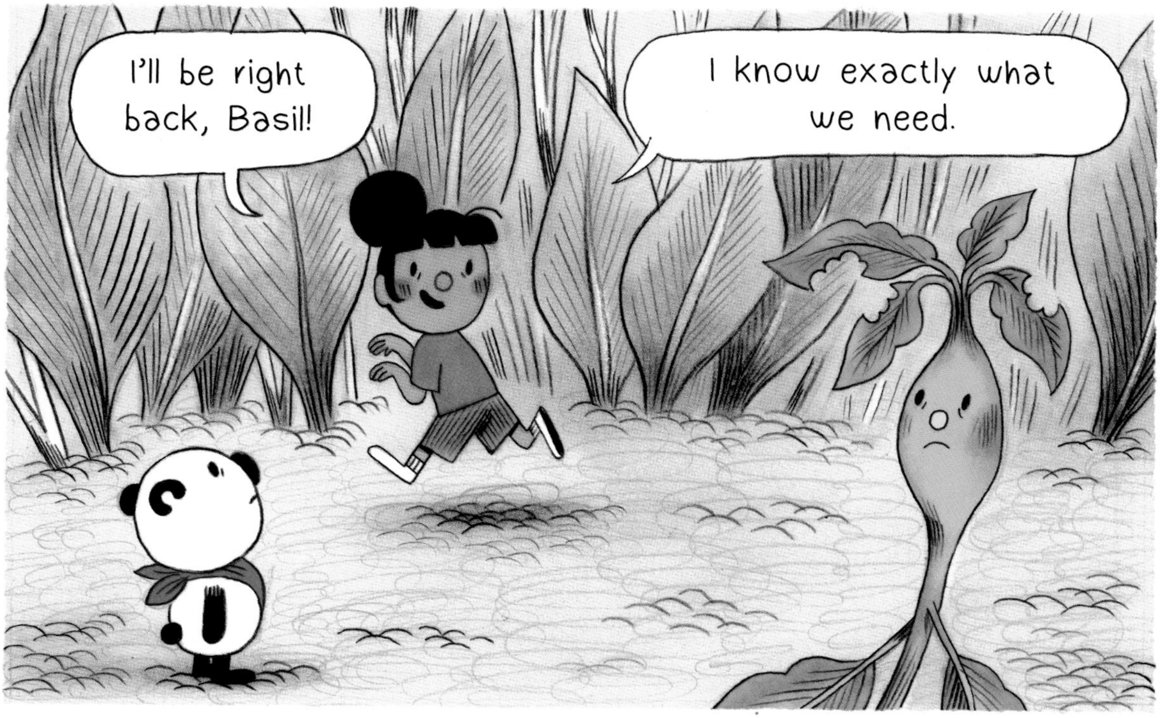
I'll be right back, Basil!
I know exactly what we need.

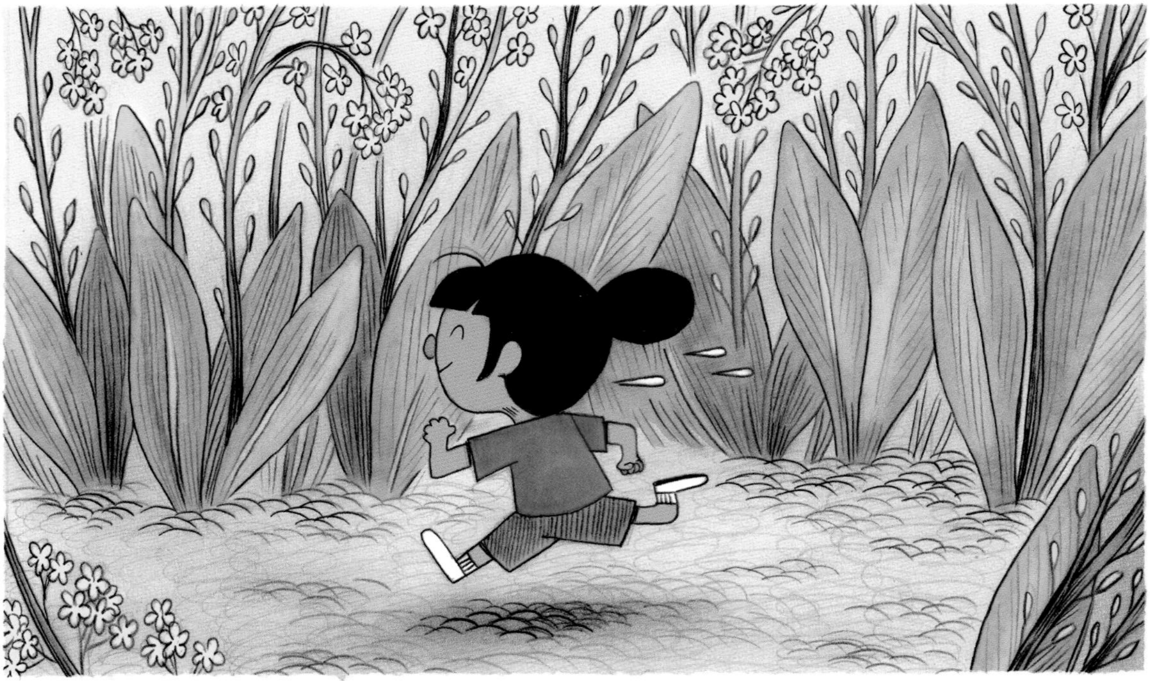

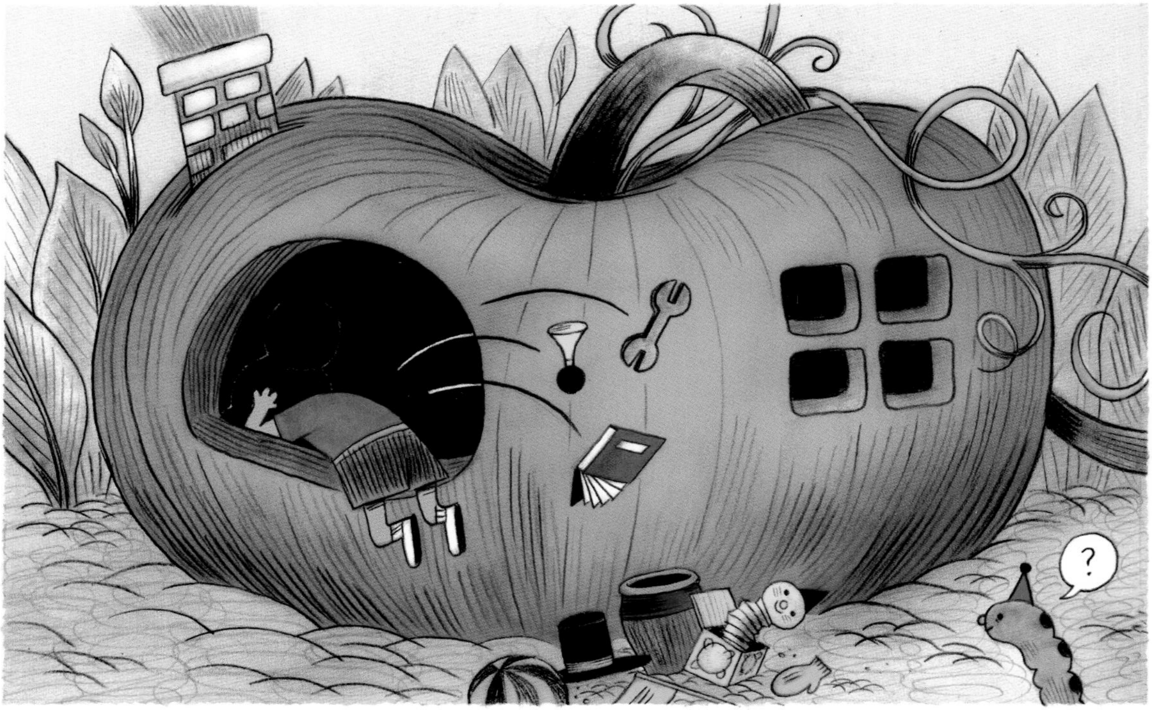
?

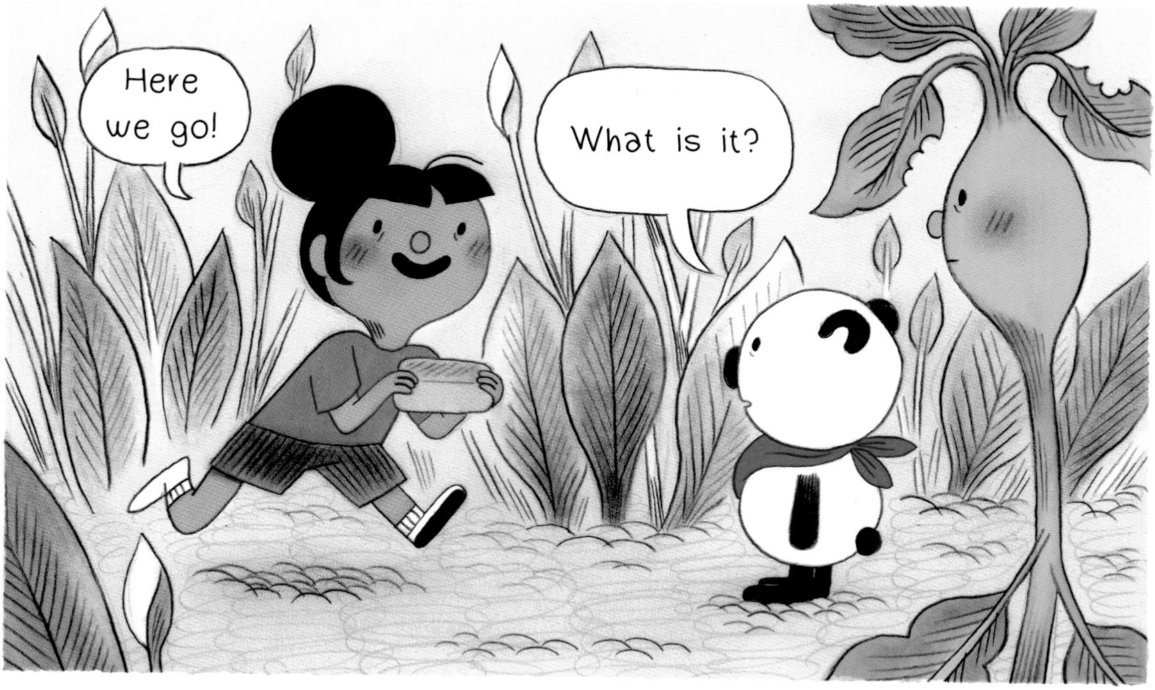
Here we go!
What is it?

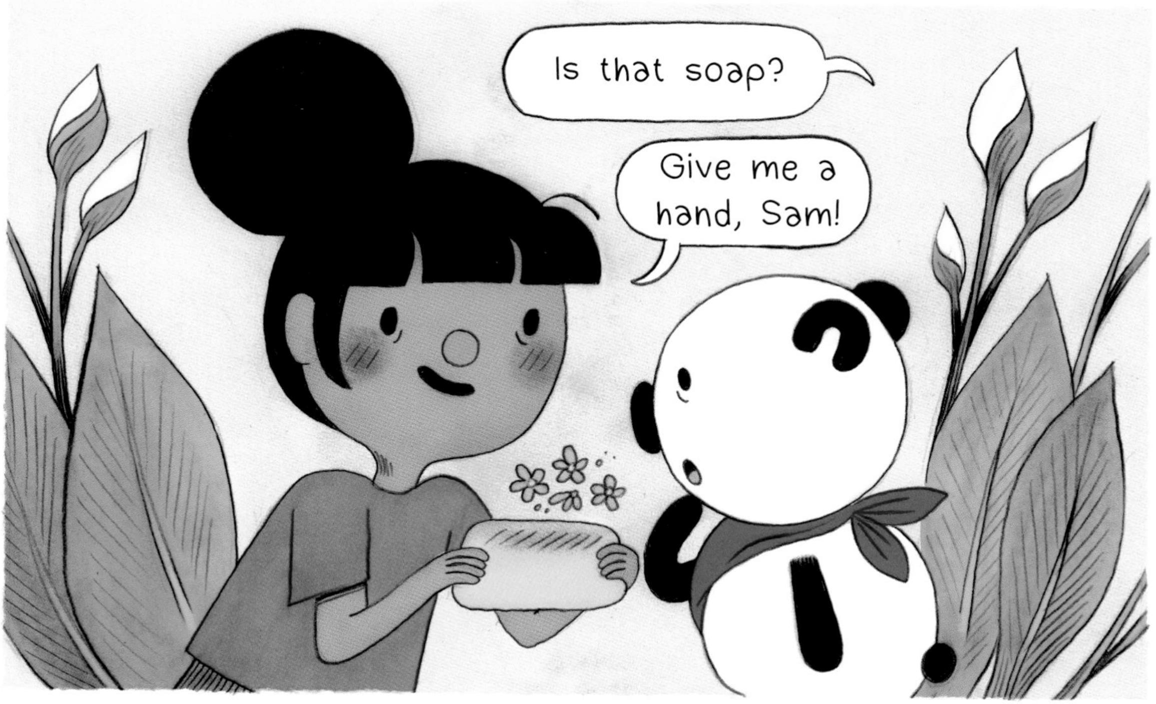
Is that soap?
Give me a hand, Sam!

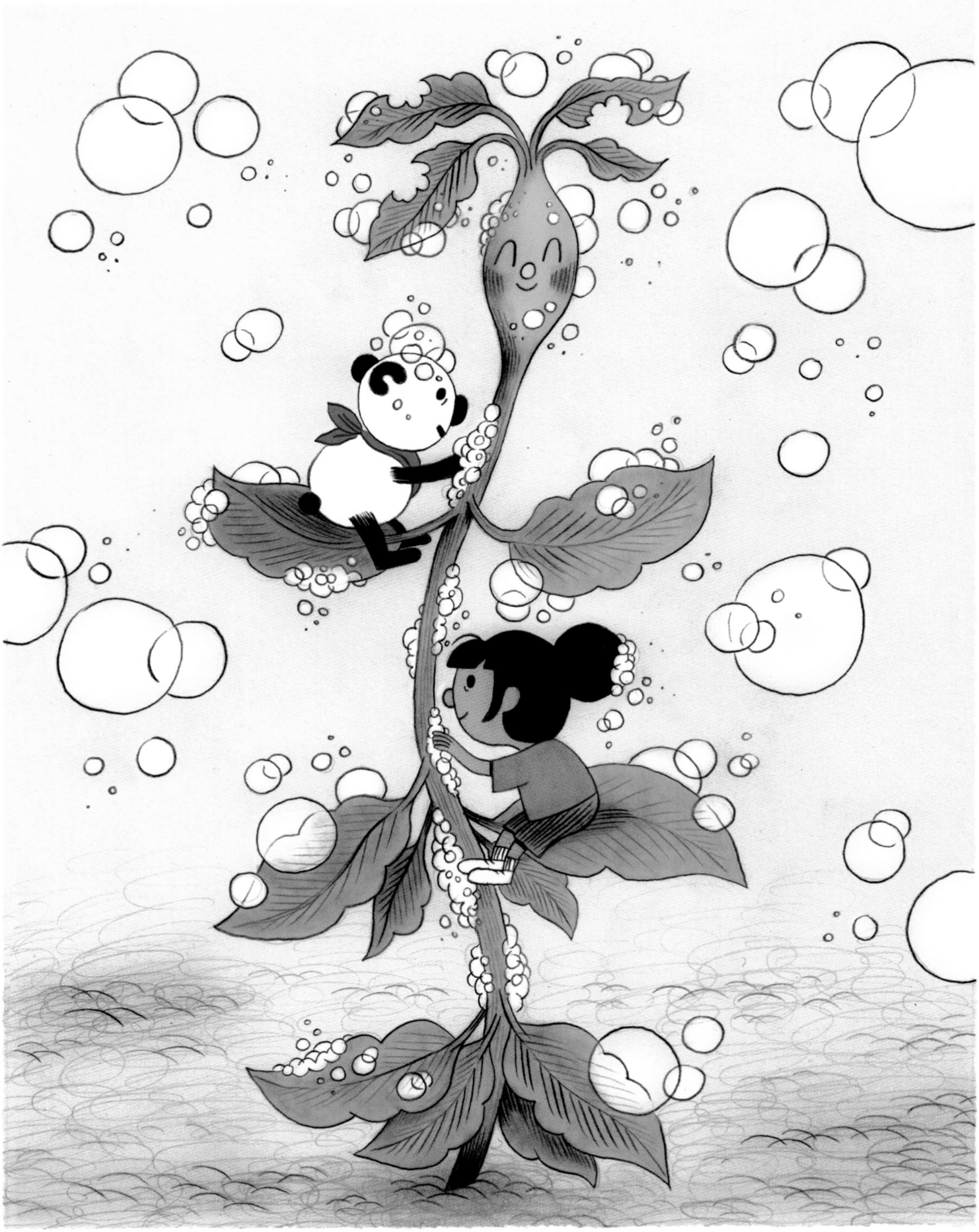

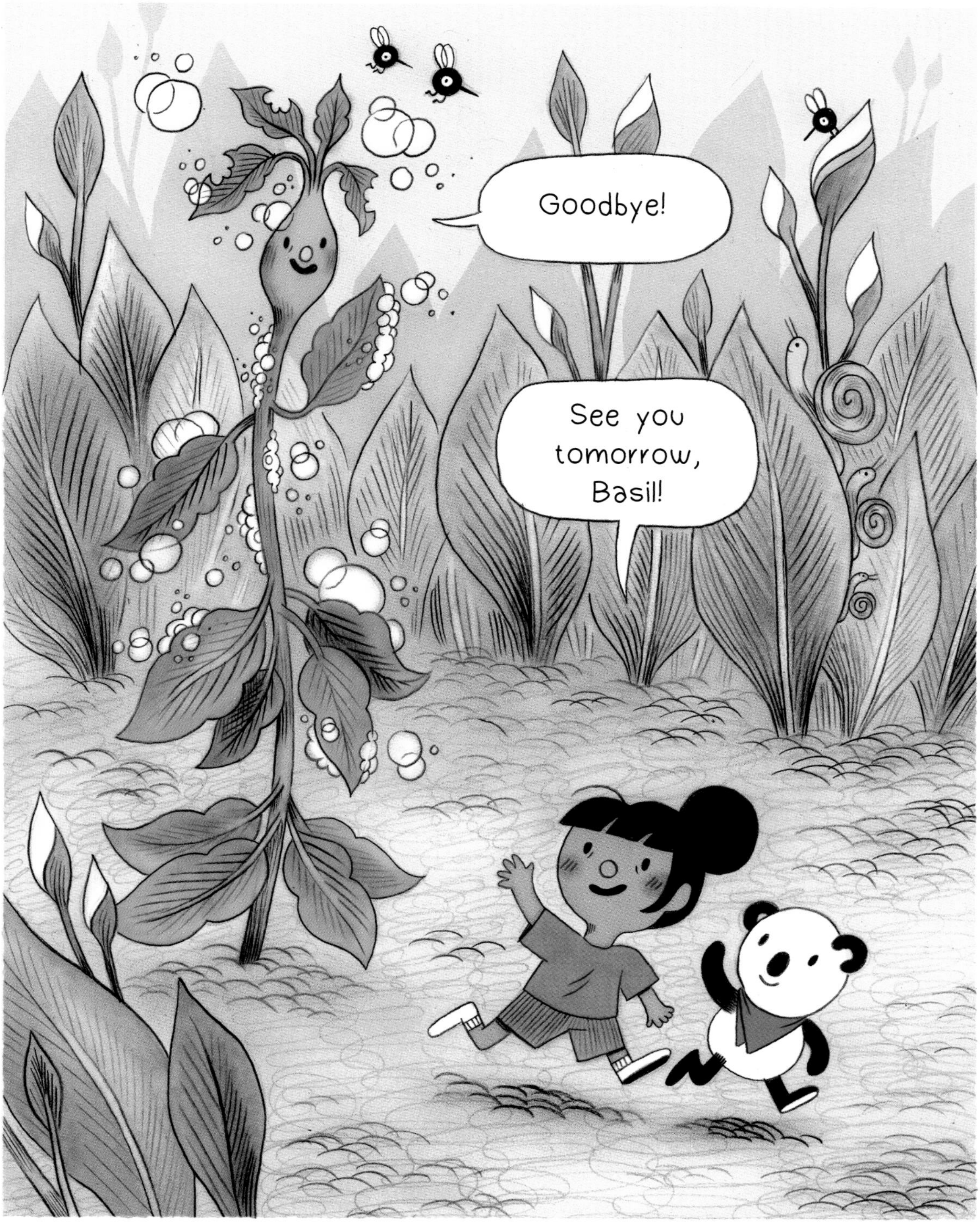
Goodbye!
See you tomorrow, Basil!

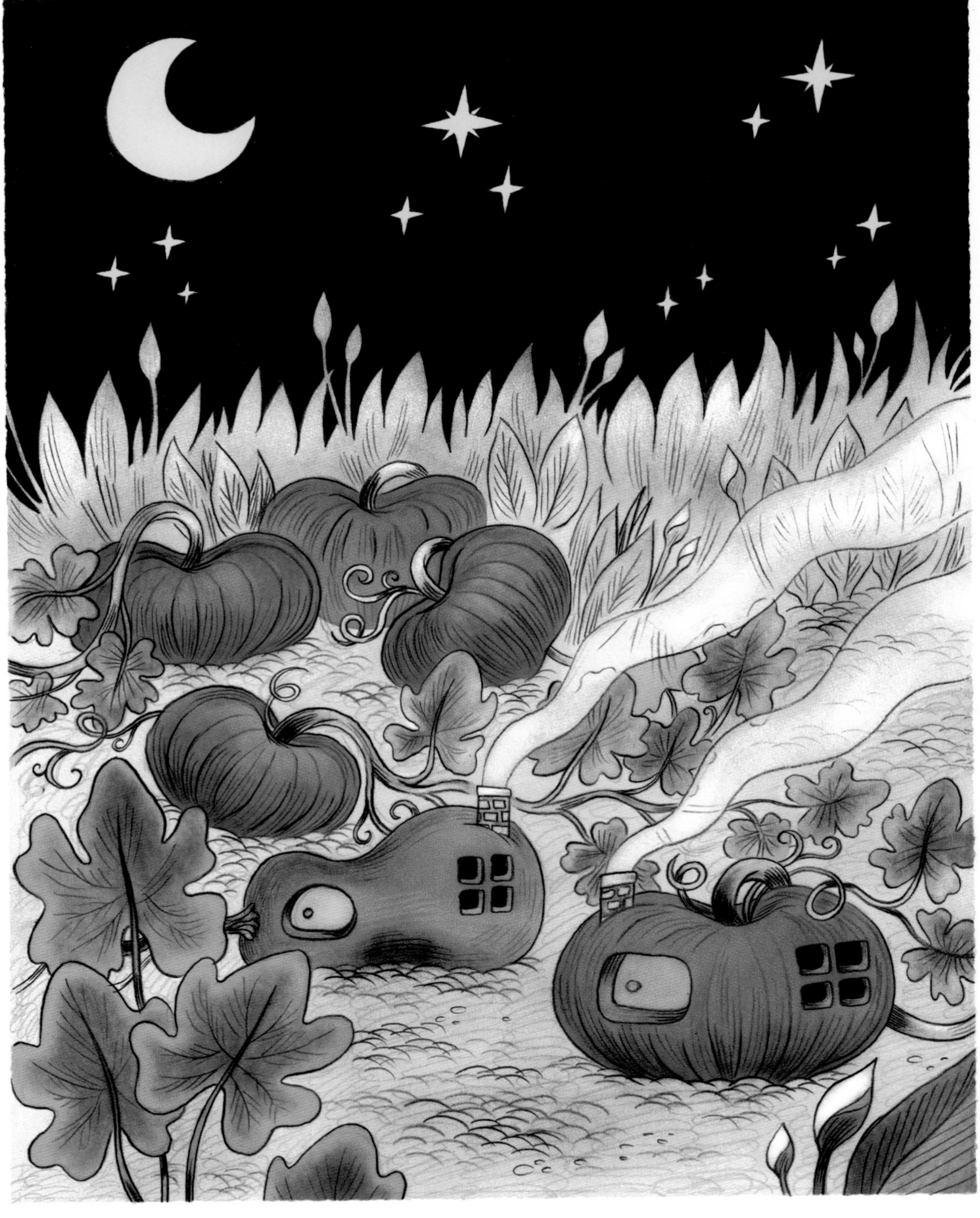

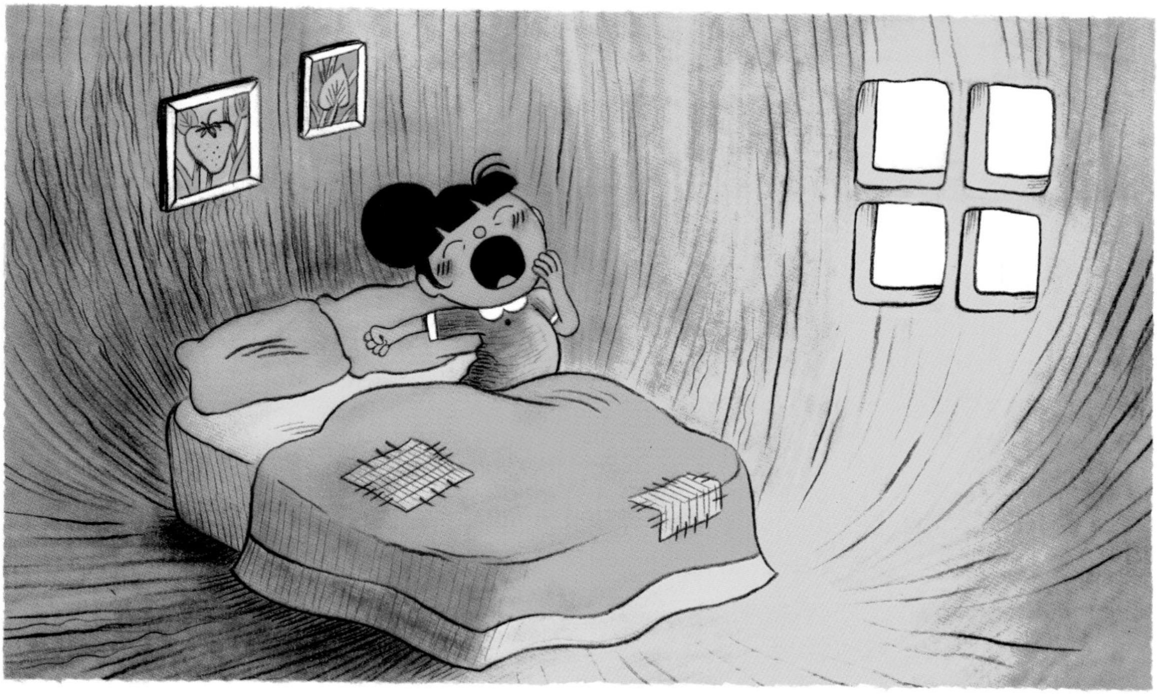

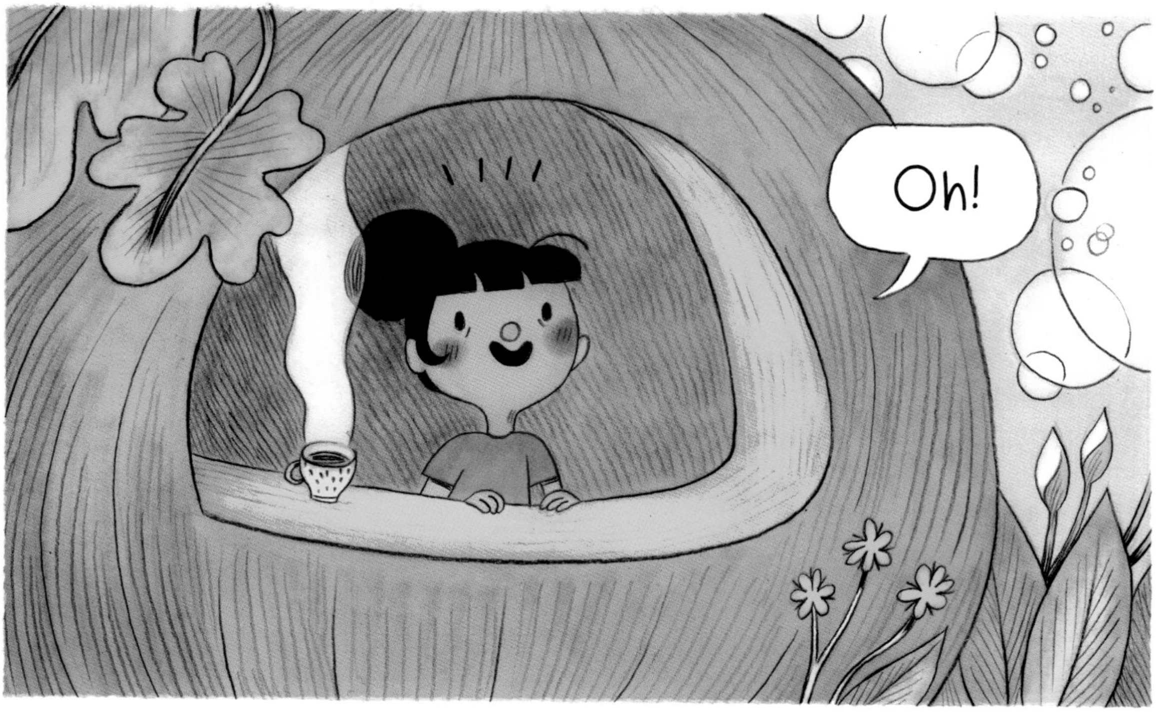
Oh!

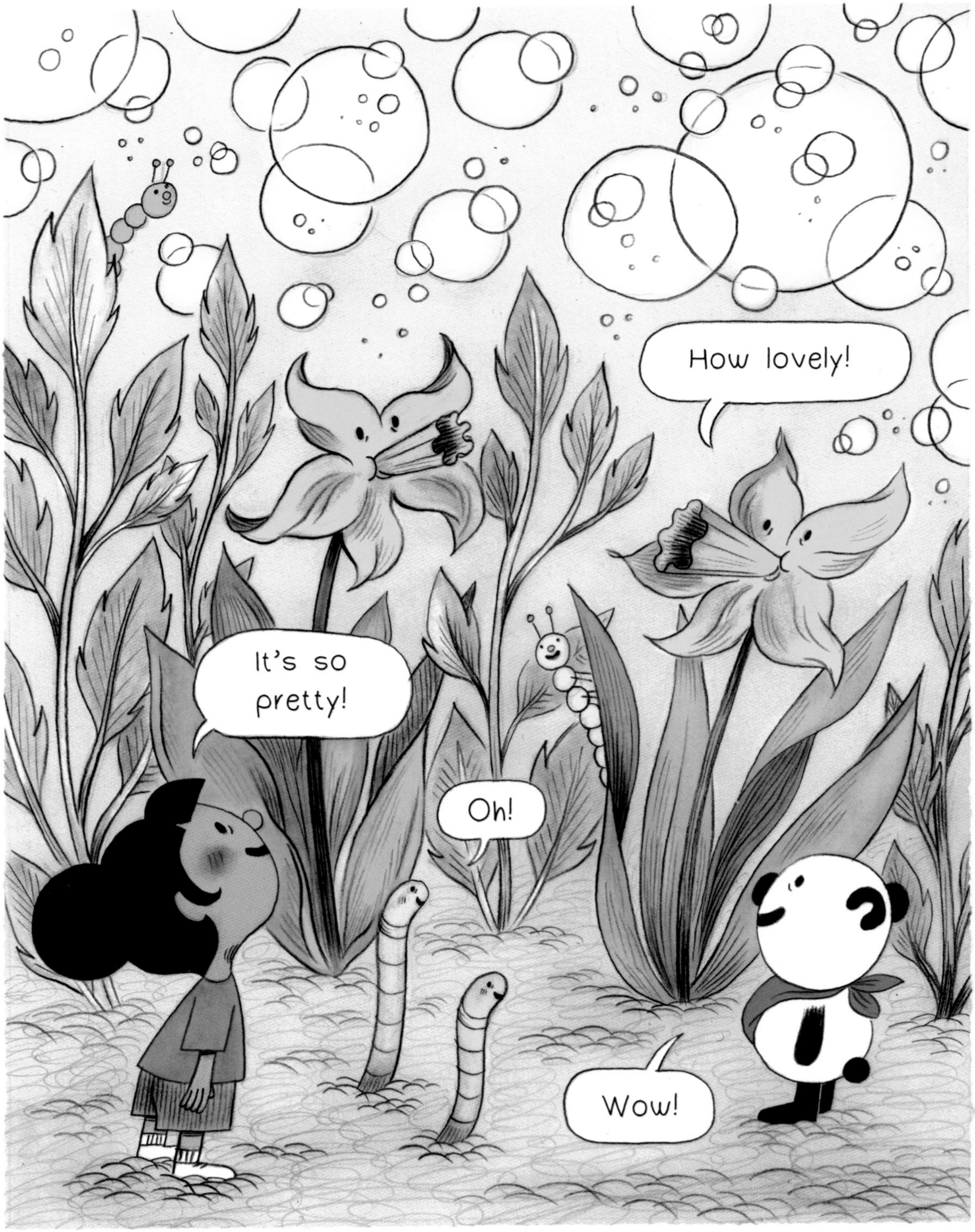
How lovely!
It's so pretty!
Oh!
Wow!

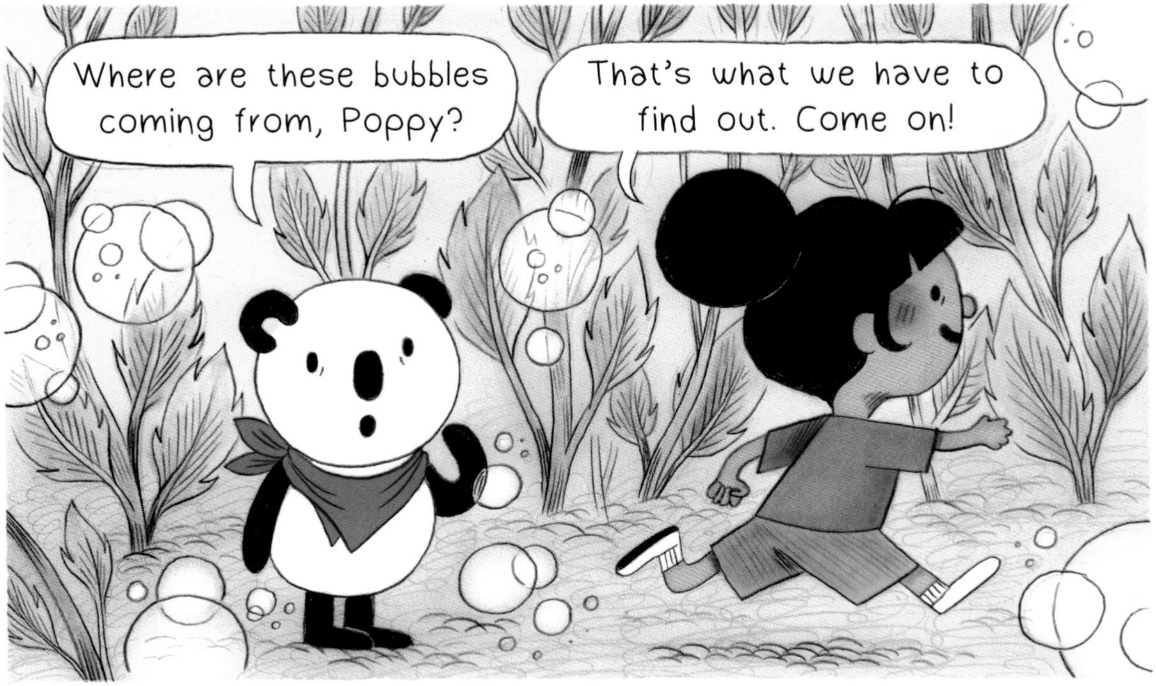
Where are these bubbles coming from, Poppy?
That's what we have to find out. Come on!

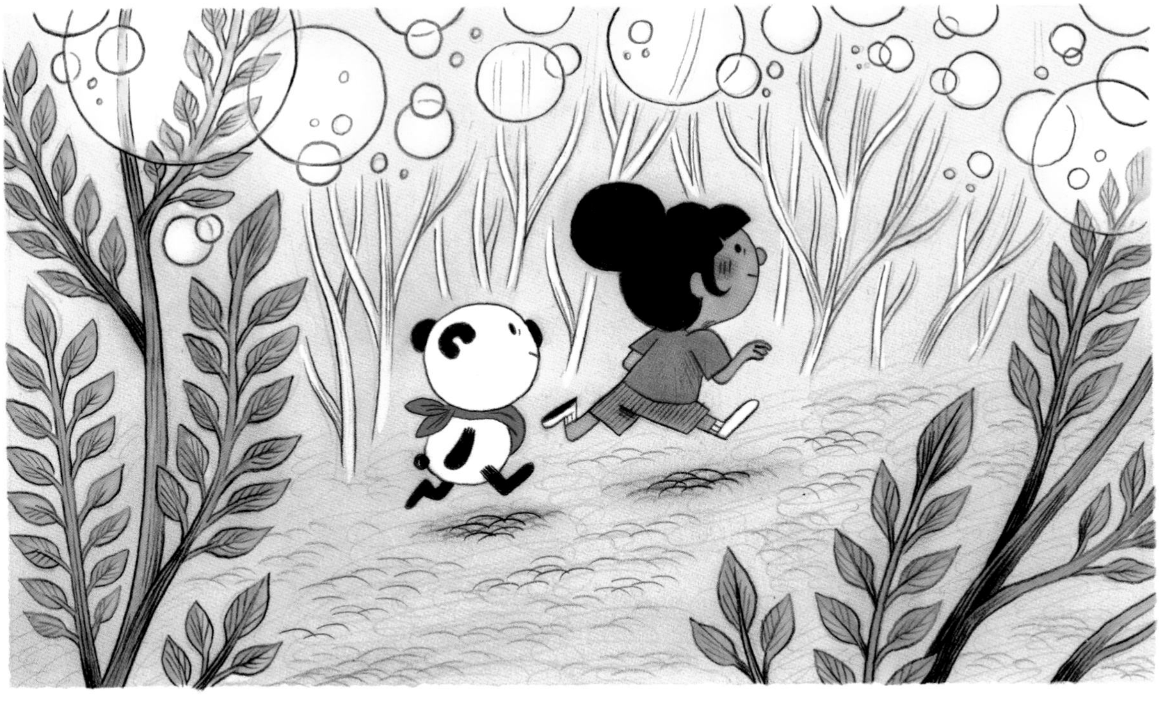

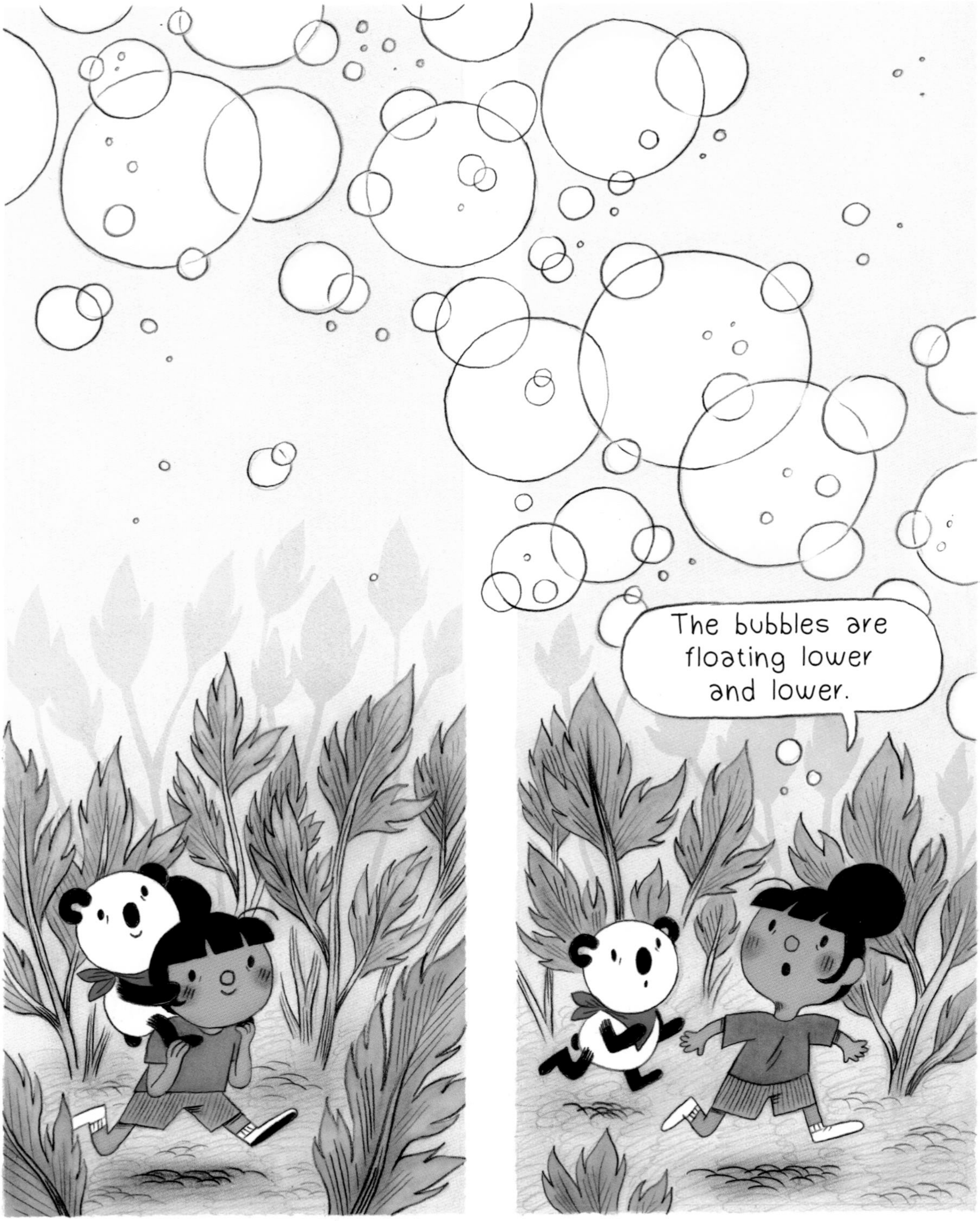
The bubbles are floating lower and lower.

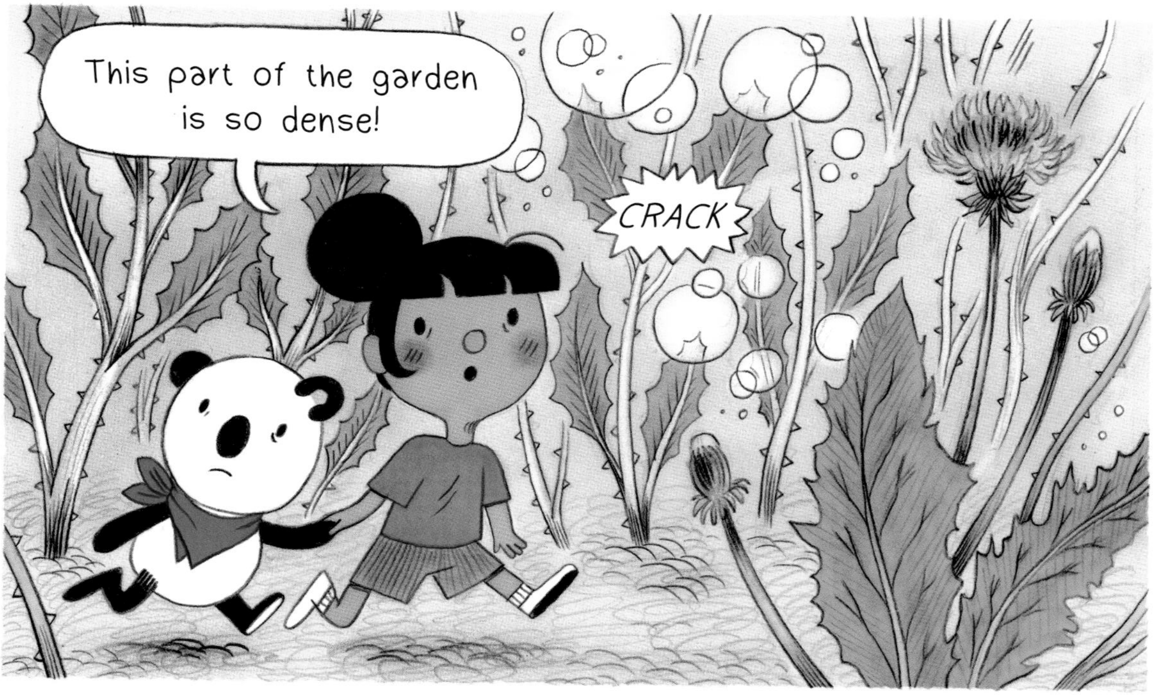
This part of the garden is so dense!
CRACK

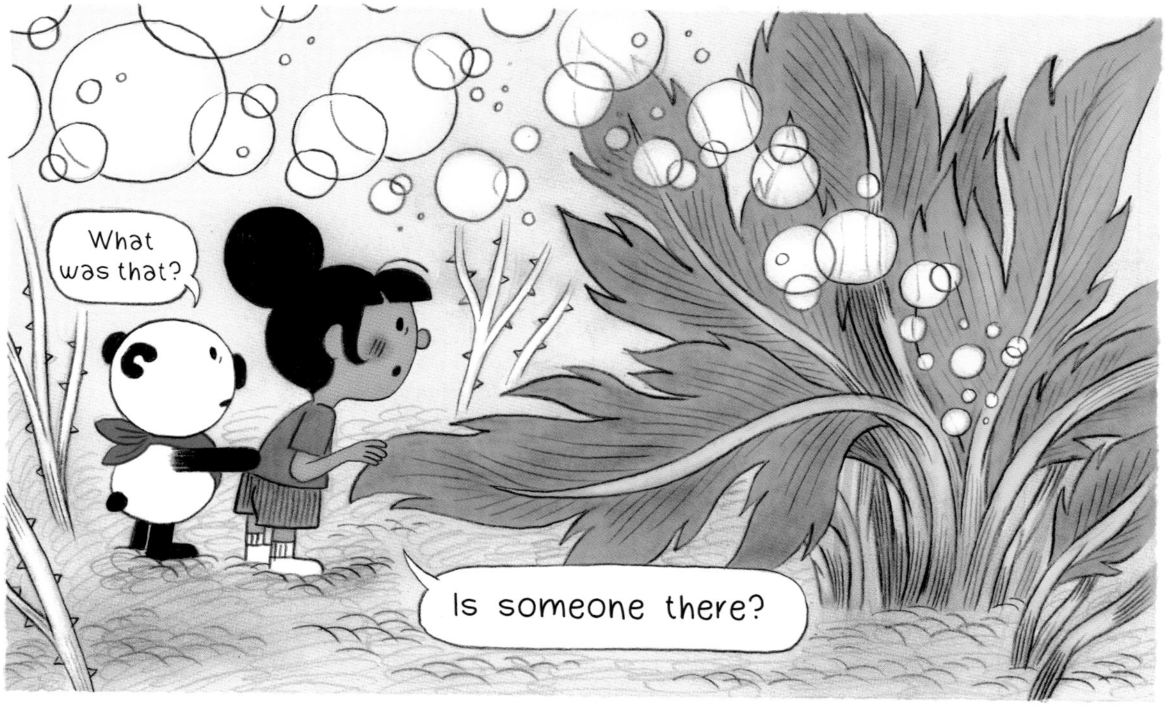
What was that?
Is someone there?

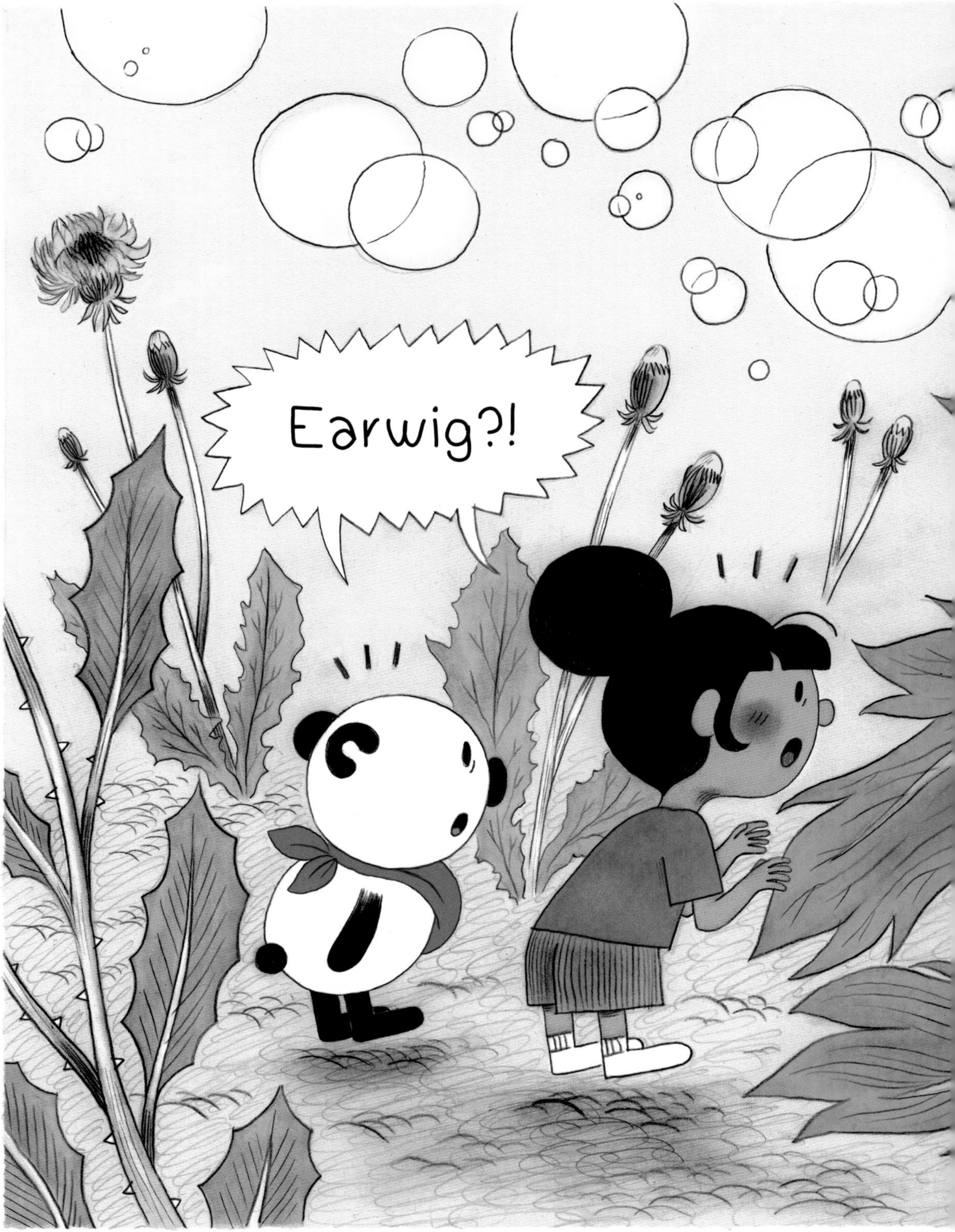
Earwig?!

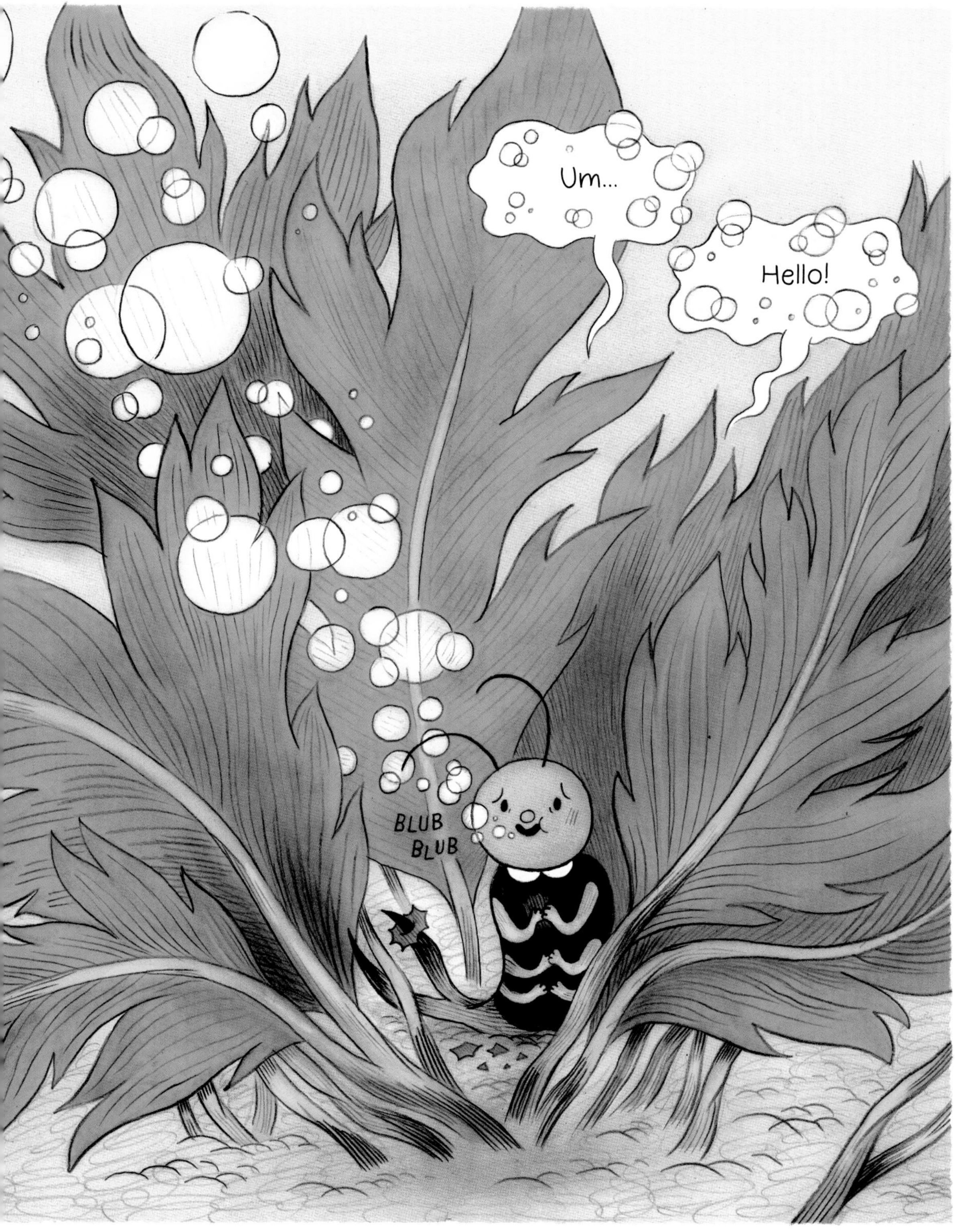
Um...
Hello!
BLUB
BLUB

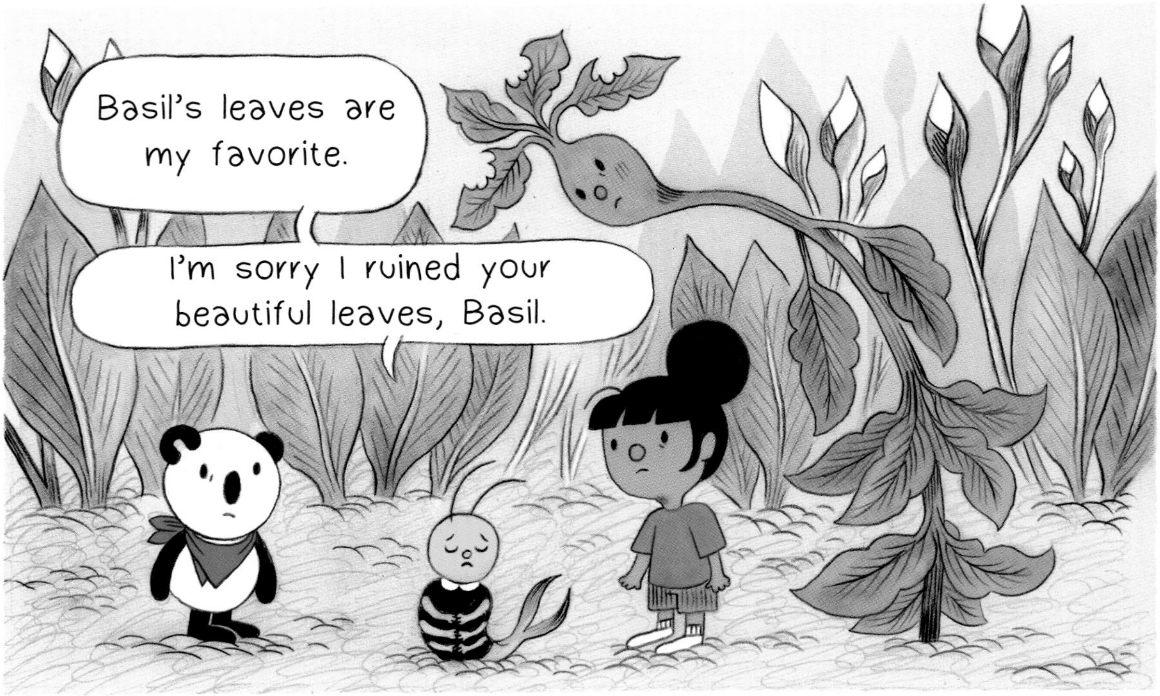
Basil's leaves are my favorite.
I'm sorry I ruined your beautiful leaves, Basil.

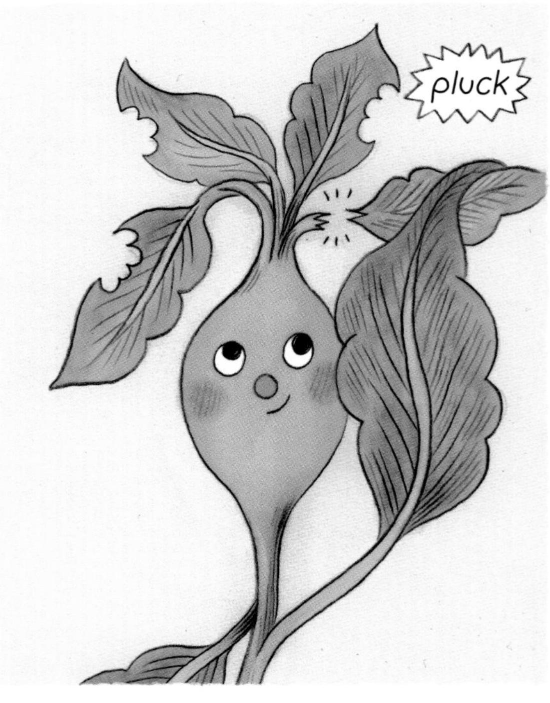
pluck

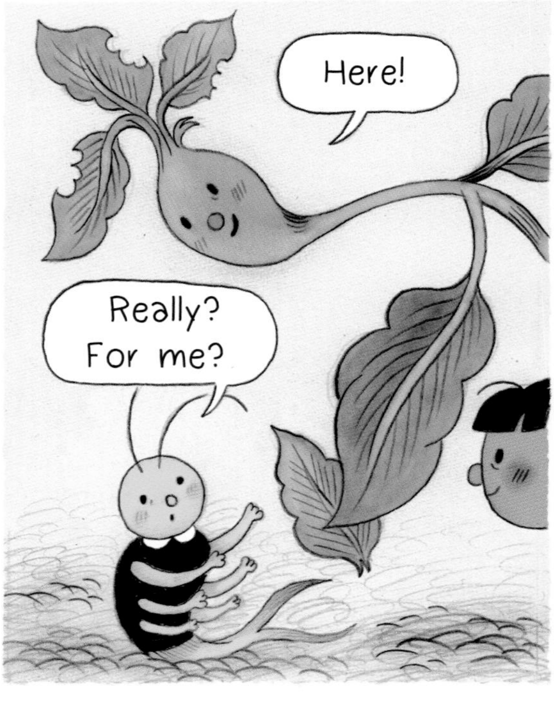
Here!
Really? For me?

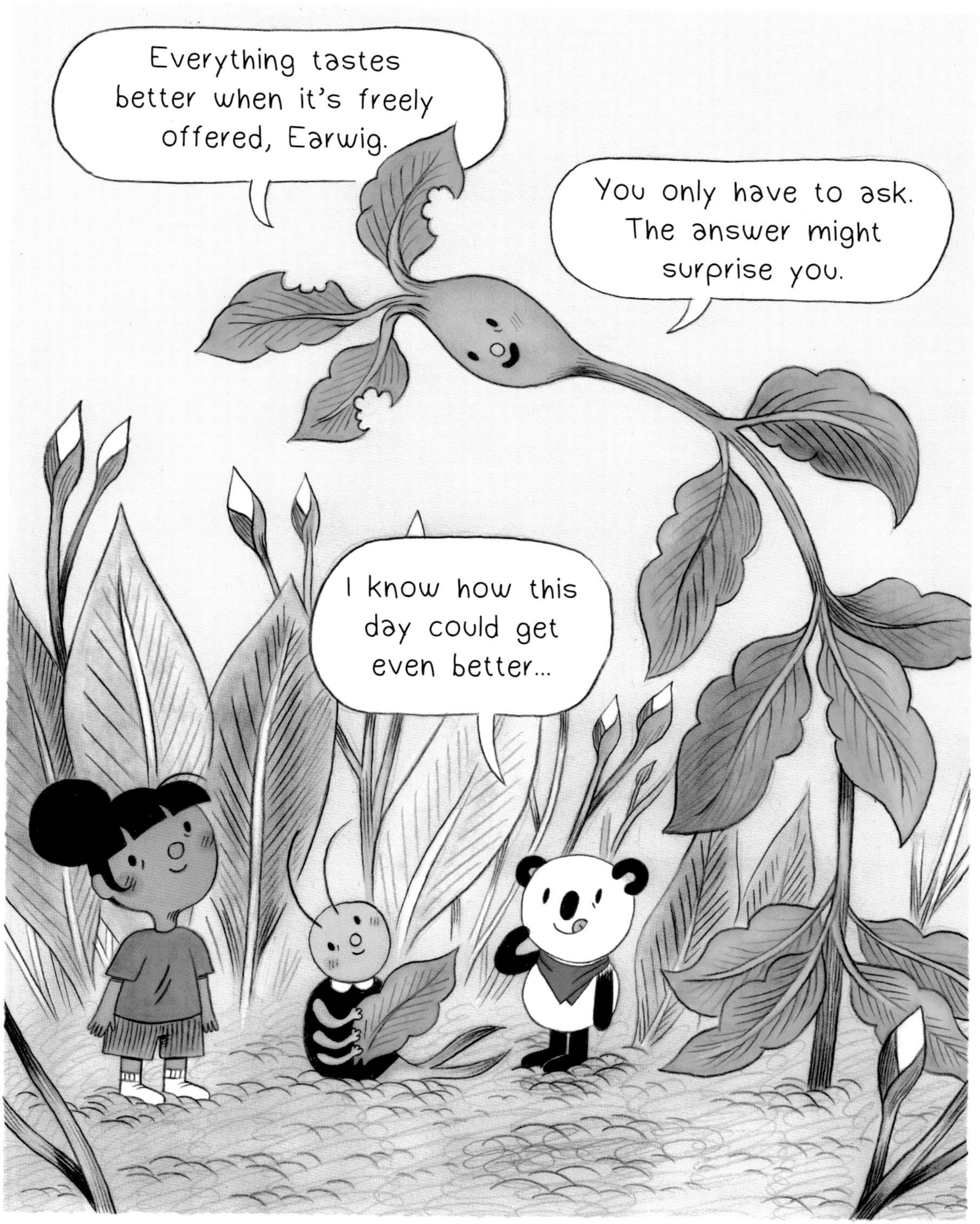
Everything tastes better when it's freely offered, Earwig.
You only have to ask. The answer might surprise you.
I know how this day could get even better...

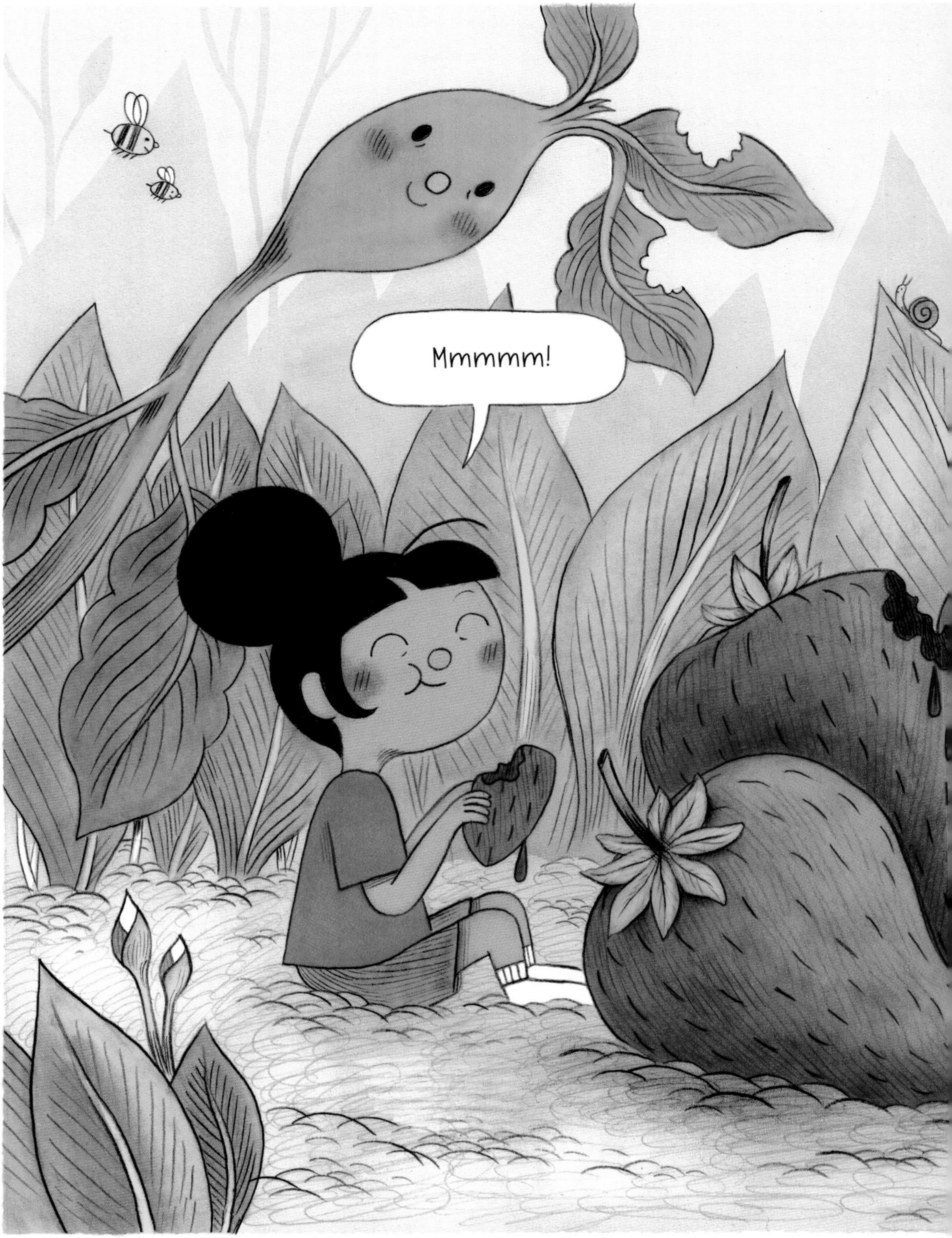
Mmmmm!

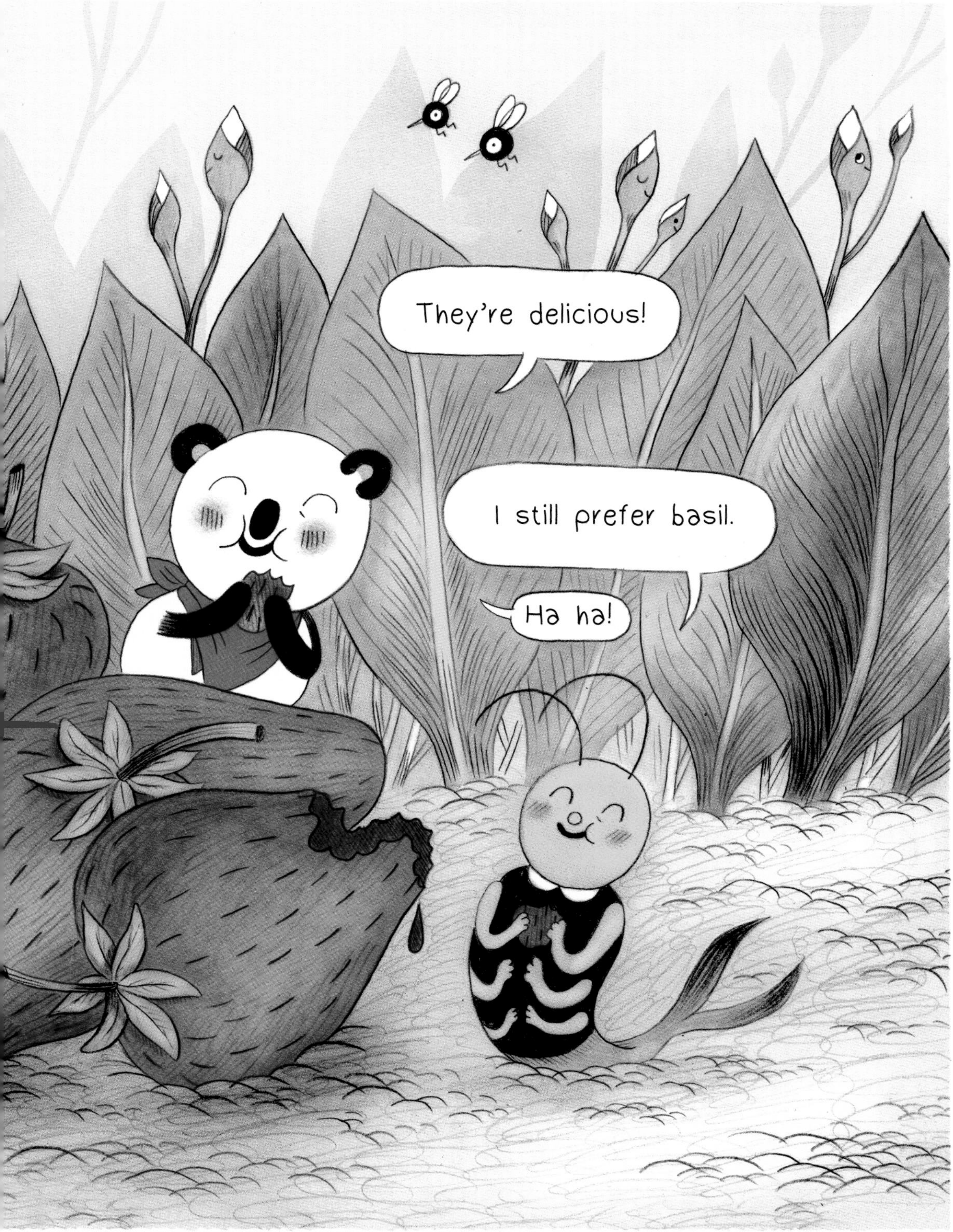
They're delicious!
I still prefer basil.
Ha ha!

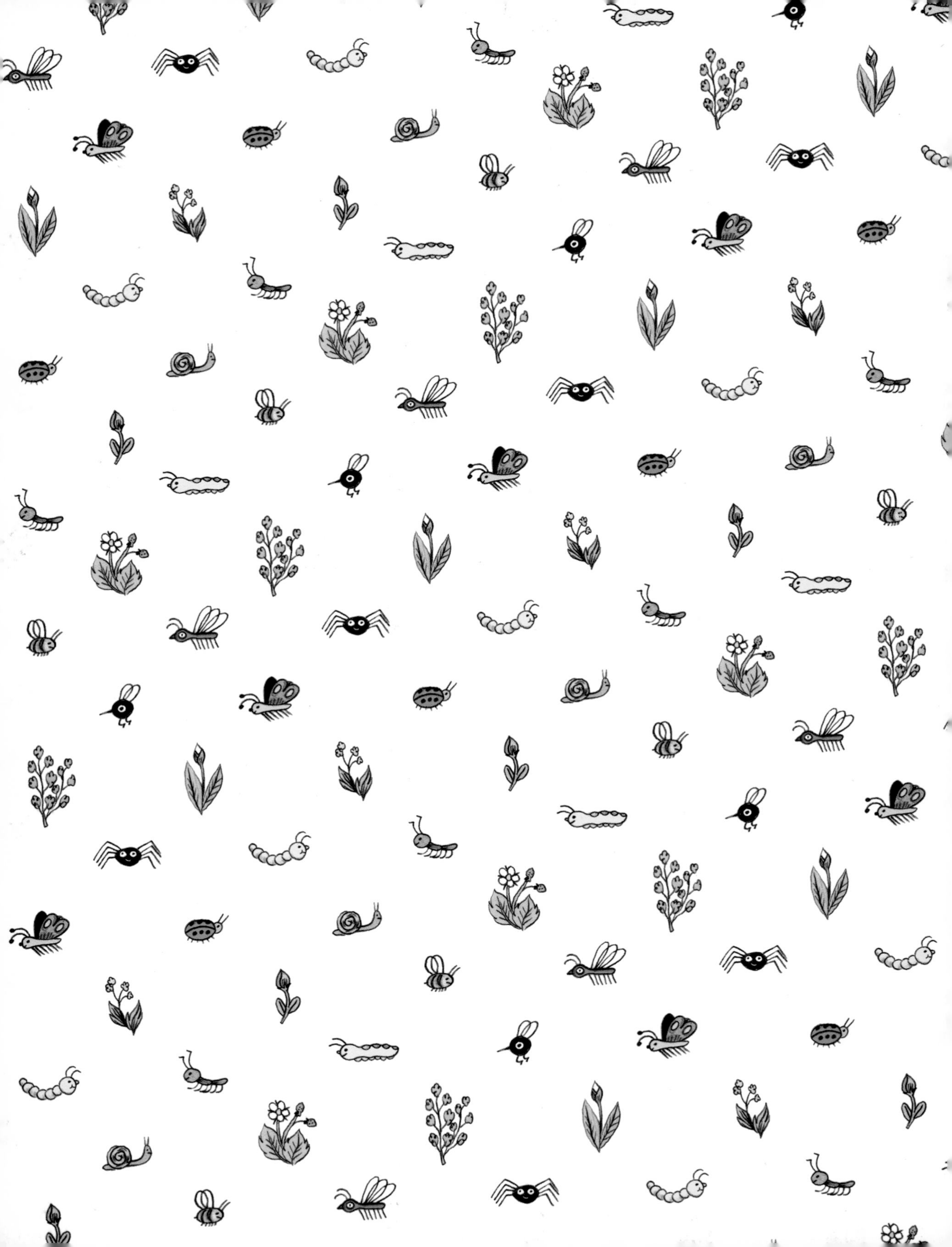